# THE LAST DUEL

# THE LAST DUEL

## JENNIFER M. FULFORD

The Musketeer Series, Book Three
Inspired by *The Three Musketeers*
By Alexandre Dumas

Book One: *Blood, Love and Steel, A Musketeer's Tale*
Book Two: *Athos & Milady, In the Beginning*

Black Bomb Books LLC
Asheville, North Carolina, USA
www.BlackBombBooks.com
blackbombbooks@gmail.com
Copyright © 2019 Jennifer M. Fulford
First Edition, March 2019



Interior layout by Maggie Powell Designs,
www.maggiepowelldesigns.com

ISBN 978-0-9980-116-7-7

*For Daryl*

# CONTENTS

# Pierre Tremon
Nicole's servant and
secret nephew,
Athos's apprentice,
Hannah's lover

### Vachon
Pierre's nemesis,
brother of Henri, who
was killed by Pierre

### Jeanne
Parisian peasant and
prostitute, Pierre's
benefactor

### Hannah
Pierre's lover,
Nicole's servant,
mother of baby Sophia

# Athos
Musketeer for Louis XIII,
Nicole's lover,
Pierre's mentor

### Father Grignan
Athos's spiritual guide,
friend of Nicole and
Pierre

### Camille
swordsman for hire,
ally of Athos

### Jussac and Biscarat
Guards for Cardinal
Richelieu, sworn
competitors of Athos

### Longdac
Musketeer sergeant
and agent of Athos

# Nicole Rieux
Comtess de Rochefort,
Athos's lover,
Pierre's defender,
Sibonne's sister

### Comte de Rochefort
husband of Nicole,
Pierre's detractor,
killed by Pierre

### Geneviève
the Comte's mistress,
arch enemy of Nicole
and Pierre

### Remi
Pierre's father and lover of
Sibonne, whose suicidal
death haunts Nicole

### Sibonne
Nicole's late sister,
Remi's lover,
Pierre's mother

### Odile
benevolent nun, savior
of Nicole

# SACRIFICES

1

# Forsaken

Wails and moans filled his waking moments. From far-off chambers at all hours, the wretchedness of human suffering reached Pierre's isolated corner of Hell. Men screeched in ways not seemingly possible, their screams intermingling with the sound of whips and torture devices he could only imagine. Stretchers. Bleeders. Iron contraptions designed to cage and maim. The whippings were the worst, slapped in successive unforgiving strikes that seemed to go on forever. Rats scurried at his feet with the spoils of the dead. The stone walls around him secreted a vile fluid, and the thick smell of rot clung to his nose hairs. Each echo from the dim chambers inside the Bastille slowly disintegrated Pierre's sanity and sank his spirit lower than damnation.

Between filthy fingers, he clutched a dot of a pebble and scratched the driest patch of wall near a soggy pile of hay, an excuse for a bed, not slept on for weeks. With the pebble, he made the tiniest of scratches. It was impossible to do more. He'd counted seventy-six days chained to the wall, shackled so long he rarely felt more than a tingle in his shoulders and wrists. Limbs above his head, the blood settled into his ribs. His cuffs hung from a spike in the wall, allowing him only to kneel. In his darker thoughts, he wished for a sharp puncture to drain away his misery.

But no torturer ever came, only a hooded hunchback who unshackled him once a day for a few minutes and tossed him a hunk of moldy bread. Those visits marked time. The hunchback was a timepiece. And after Pierre gobbled the ration down and savoured the brief respite from his restraints, he scratched the wall.

One more day.

His captivity had been far longer than seventy-six days. But he'd been dumb. Denial kept him from counting the first few weeks. Or months? Someone would come, he had once believed. His plight smacked of theatrics, bad behaviour that now required a show of authority by the powerful French aristocracy.

Daily, he replayed his last memories of freedom that last night in Paris. Sometimes, he replayed them every hour. He couldn't erase them: a bloody sword, the eyes of Parisian society on him, revenge complete, then guards and chains, Nicole shrieking his name in Le Louvre above the shocked aristocrats, as he was dragged through a gawking crowd into the dark night of Paris and to the cold dingy labyrinth few survived—the Bastille.

Pierre relished the memory of the slumped body of the Comte de Rochefort in a pool of blood. It meted out revenge he'd waited a lifetime to achieve as a loathsome servant of the Comte, who had belittled him at every chance. Not his first kill—but the one that mattered most. The kill that altered his life.

Triumphantly decadent. And … stupid.

His disposability as a French citizen took hold almost immediately, the same time he lost his freedom and mobility.

The chains were meant to break his spirit. He'd gone from a dank cell, his initial holding spot, to a lightless passageway where few bothered to pass. Just the hunchback. And the noise from the nearby killing chambers.

He suppressed the urge to scream. Today, waiting for the hunchback, his will seemed smaller than ever. At least he had managed to escape real torture. But his stomach jittered at any small sound that remotely resembled a footstep. Dread set him on edge. The hunchback had a limp, so his gait was recognizable. A long dash and a thump. A long dash and a thump. The approach made Pierre's mouth water.

The squeal of a hinge sounded in a far-off corner. Pierre squinted tightly to accentuate his hearing. Unmistakable. Boots with heels. Two heavy feet. Not the familiar dash and thump. The stalking boots rounded a corner and another. Pierre buried his chin into his chest. The echoes vanquished his hope. Today, he prayed, his morbid status as the forgotten might continue.

∞∞∞

At the Rue Férou, Athos tracked down the buxom hostess of his previous Paris quarters.

"We threw out your things with the dung," she said, almost spitted, when he asked about the few items he'd left in his Paris apartment countless months ago. For a mademoiselle who had once cast comely glances his way, he found her turnabout disheartening.

Not that his possessions mattered anymore. He wished he'd had sense enough to entrust some items to d'Artagnan. His prized sword. A casket of wine. Probably sold for a few pistoles or traded for one wild night of revelry. But now, his most prized possessions were nowhere near Paris; they were not possessions—but people.

He paid the young woman the rents he owed and asked for his room back.

"Hardly," she said, stomping up the stairs. "For you, the attic."

He relented. At least it had a small writing desk.

From his bags, he found a stash of paper and a charcoal and started his first letter. He missed Nicole and the intimacy they'd carved out in Rochefort far more than he thought he would.

*My love,*

*I've arrived in Paris in record time. The spring weather cooperated. My room and few personal items are intact, and I will write again once I've tracked down a willing soul to grant my entrance to the Bastille. A certain serenity passes through me as I often weightlessly think of you. You fill me with greater purpose. Please rest and take care. Rejoice in the oncoming arrival of our child. I send my unending love and hope. Know that I will succeed. Pierre will be free, and so shall we. Your devoted servant, Athos*

Typical of his nature, Athos couldn't rest. On the ride eastward from Rochefort to Paris, he'd caught naps in the woods when overwhelming exhaustion bore down. Now that he'd arrived in the city, he had a singular purpose: do anything within his power to free Pierre, Nicole's only nephew.

His first stop was the abbey of Saint Germain-de-Prés. Trying to look official, he wore his blue doublet and his Musketeer tabard emblazoned with the King's seal. A monk in the abbey informed him Father Simon Grignan had gone into hiding.

"Hiding?"

"Unfortunately, yes," the monk nodded and frowned. "After the death of the Comte de Rochefort, rumours reached here that Father Grignan would be implicated. Without telling any of us, he disappeared one night. No one has seen him since a few days after the Comte's funeral mass. You're the first to inquire. Do you have any information about him?"

Athos shook his head. "Did he leave a note? A clue to his state of mind?"

"None," the monk said. "But we do have letters that came afterward. Several arrived for him in the months after his disappearance."

It didn't take much convincing for the monk to hand over the small stack. Included in the bundle were the letters Athos had sent to Grignan from Rochefort in the previous months. Their efforts to reach the sympathetic priest were for naught. The storied hope he had placed on Grignan as a possible go-between for Pierre's release disappeared in less than a minute.

"Will you find him for us?" the monk asked with a hopeful pitch in his voice.

"We shall see," Athos said and took the letters on the pledge of their return if the priest resurfaced.

Athos regretted building hope in Nicole that Pierre's future rested on the letters. They requested Grignan use his immutable good nature. But in French politics, even the pious couldn't escape being drawn into sordid circumstances, and in their case, epic ones.

The story of Nicole's husband, though a contemptible figure among his peers, gave the rich and poor a good tale to retell. The demise of the Comte de Rochefort would be repeated by successive generations. The Comte's audacious public death by a vengeful servant swept up many decent people in its details. Athos shouldered his accountability in the affair, by unintentionally falling in love with the Comtesse. Even gossip couldn't embellish more than the simple facts. No wonder the priest had vanished into thin air.

Leaving the abbey, the spring air chilled Athos from the inside out. Freeing Pierre, the nephew Nicole had concealed as her servant, had just gotten more complicated.

∞ ∞ ∞ ∞

"Are you warm enough?" Hannah brought an extra shawl with her into the chapel outside the château.

Nicole sat mesmerized by the candle flames. She'd lit one every day since Athos's departure for Paris weeks ago. Two other candles burned in vigil for Pierre and her unborn child. Her belly, firm and ripening, gave her reason to hope and brace against the loneliness.

"I'm fine," she said, forcing a small smile toward her servant.

"Baby Sophia is so strong now. Have you seen how she pulls on my skirts? I worry she'll grab a hot coal from the hearth. It would be just like her, taking after Pierre."

Nicole rubbed Hannah's hand. The two women sat in the chapel, enveloped in quiet.

"Everyone in the château is worried about you," Hannah said, quieter than normal.

"Unnecessarily so," Nicole said and squeezed the warm fingers beneath hers.

"You're so alone. Again."

"Less so now that I have Athos."

"But he's gone." Hannah heaved a sigh, maybe in regret of her bluntness. Her immaturity played against her.

Nicole rubbed her tummy, where she centered her attention, or distracted it. "I have so much, even if he's not here."

Hannah shrugged. "And when he finds my Pierre, I suppose I'll have reason to forgive him."

"I should hope so. Athos felt only fondness for him."

"Will he find him?" Hannah's plea had been asked countless times since Pierre's capture.

"If it is God's will," Nicole answered again.

The candles blazed and shortened until Hannah tired of the contemplation and left Nicole to her thoughts.

Every well of her patience was low. Five months with child. A widow. In a love affair with a Musketeer. Shunned by Court. Her reputation might never be washed clean. Her husband's death at the hands of her nephew placed her in legendary infamy. So far, the price had been worth it, if her love of Athos bore out. She believed they were a perfect match. As elemental as water to earth.

Being apart from him was a necessary sadness. She pondered if he felt the same loss in her absence and knew that he did. Pierre's survival required sacrifice. Feeling sorry for her situation seemed self-indulgent. She must wait and let God, and her lover, work miracles.

She rose from the pew and stood until the last candle went out.

# 2

# A Chance

Pierre dreamed of Hannah. He lay naked beside her in the grass of the forested land on the Comte's estate. Rochefort in full bloom was no match for her beauty. Hannah's body opened like a milkweed to expose her soft, delicate curves. His hands followed the fine textures of her shape, up her torso to the peaks of her breasts. She gave him free range. The milkiest warmth below her navel lured him down to explore the fragrance. He loved the essence of her on his lips. His tongue passed across her most secret places. His lurid sinful desires and lustfulness stirred a perpetual craving in him. He wanted her more after every encounter. Each time never fulfilled him completely. They fanned a dark ember, and she rarely extinguished its growing heat.

∞∞∞

Blistered and dazed, still chained upright, Pierre twisted his shackled hands. One burned in maddening agony. The scalding he'd endured hours earlier had replaced numbness with searing pain. His brain convinced him time wouldn't cure it. Twisting his body against the damp wall, he tried laying his palms on the clammy stone. His ashen knuckles brought up memories of the powdered faces of the mesdemoiselles at Court on the day of his demise.

Shivering from scalp to toes, he moaned low and long then cursed his weakness. He had wept openly before the men who burned his hand, unable to contain the pain. He had begged for mercy from the nameless, blank bearers of torture, the devil's agents. He had plead for mercy scores of times, screaming: *Why? Why?* Then the moaning turned to wailing on the third dunk in the bucket of boiling water.

His cries drained him of precious energy. Of the few pieces of advice Athos had given him, one rule stood out. *Conserve your energy to survive a fight.* Under the Musketeer's instruction at home in the country, he'd learned much more than how to wield a sword. He learned lessons of fortitude and attitude. The difference between strength and bravado. Maybe if he had taken more heed of the elder swordsman's wisdom, his situation might be different. He wouldn't have killed a sovereign in public. Wouldn't have wanted to make himself notorious. Wouldn't have ended up forgotten. He moaned in agony despite himself.

Shuddering at the idea of their return, Pierre expected his torturers to exact much more of his hide. His head had been bagged on the way to the boiling chamber, but along the route, he had inhaled the overwhelming scent of decaying flesh. Its putridness rivaled the worst stench of dung in all of France. There was a difference between the aroma of heaps of manure and compost and that of mangy rats, human excrement, and rotting body parts. At every blind turn, the rot wafted into his lungs, confirming that the Bastille was not a prison but a den of unspeakable evil.

Hanging against the wall, he balanced his hair-trigger fear against the memories of Rochefort, weeks away by horse. He relived the dream about Hannah. It made sense that the vision ended off-kilter. *Askew. Unsatisfied.* But whether there was truth to his unsated desire was of no relevance now. Survival took precedent. Maybe his insatiable nature might play into his favour as death inched closer.

But how to survive this? The plans of the devil lay in his path. Pierre could hardly see around the in-and-out curve of the nearly black passage. A light flickered around a corner, casting a dancing strobe that could either signal hope or despair. The hunchback or the killing men. Until the scalding, he'd been spared. Or at least it seemed that way in retrospect.

Where was mercy? Where was his savior, Nicole? Athos? Hannah? God? He believed the only conclusion a man can make on the brink of madness, that he was truly alone. The sickening poison of hopelessness nested in every pocket of his darkening mind.

"Ho, there!" a voice prodded, along with a blunt end of a long pole on Pierre's shoulder.

Pierre looked up, startled. The stocky bearded man, new in Pierre's recollection, grabbed him by the cheeks and tossed his head from side to side.

"You the criminal they call Tremon?"

Pierre hadn't heard his name since Queen Anne had spoken it before the damnable act that had landed him here. He nodded.

"Then this is for you." Swiveled around, the pole bore a red hot iron. Before Pierre could react, the man yanked up the side of his shirt and jabbed the brand onto his soft flank.

His vocal burst ripped through the chambers until it caused the other wretched souls in the bowels to yell back. An act of solidarity, maybe. Recognition of futility. The sound of immeasurable suffering bonded those in bondage.

When Pierre revived, the fleur-de-lis blistered his skin white and caused the whole side of his body to sting. His jaw clenched tightly enough to strain the muscles in his neck.

The light from a side passage flickered again, and prayers floated in on the draft. From one end, the captives were repeating *Hail Mary, full of grace, Hail Mary, full of grace*. Most of the new prisoners still had hope, a voice, a will. Not Pierre. Not now. Perhaps never again.

Two men—a guard and a robed figure—stepped into the wet passageway, the place he wasted away. In far too much pain, he never heard the telltale footsteps.

A measured voice asked, "Is this the one?"

A grunt confirmed it.

"So, you are the one who wanted to make a name for yourself to the Queen of France?" Pierre, blind from pain, strained to see the speaker. A pot-bellied figure dressed like a priest, face hidden beneath a dark hood, stretched out his hand to offer him something. A man of the clergy, among the forsaken. Pierre shook his head, delusional.

*Hail Mary, full of grace*. The steady chants kept time to the throbbing in his hand and side. Pierre refocused on the object in the priest's hand: a dull red apple, bruised and decaying at the stem.

Pierre weakly rattled his chains, and the guard unlocked him. Faint, he nearly fell onto his knees but fumbled for the priest's hands. He caught the fruit between his forearms and chest while the priest chattered reflectively.

"He was notorious overnight, then forsaken."

Pierre swallowed the first mushy bite. His response was weak: "Forsaken?"

The priest nodded to the side. "Why, yes. Paris has a fickle memory."

"How long?" He nodded once between bites.

The priest removed his hood—his warm eyes, framed by graying temples and a matching beard, glowed a little. "Three months shy of a year."

Shy of a year, irreplaceable life, lost. A year in his daughter's life. A year without touching Hannah. Days that had actually grown to months.

He nearly dropped the apple in a puddle of waste. The priest knelt and curled a large hand around the next bite. "Don't let this go for naught," he said and looked intently into the broken young man, the expression conveying something more. "You must never lose your will to live."

He brought the apple to Pierre's mouth and helped him take another bite. Astonished by the priest's unusual gesture, he blinked and complied. His teeth struck something hard. Pierre held the apple to his mouth and breathed in the realization. He smelled freedom. In another desperate bite, a key slipped from the rotten core into his trembling palm.

Nodding, the priest waved another direction along the route, an obvious tactic to distract the guard.

"I may return tomorrow with a final sacrament for the doomed," the clergy told the guard. The priest tightened his lips, and the guard re-cuffed Pierre before the two shuffled away.

# Freedom and Capture

Rather than waste his time tracking the priest, Athos had no choice but to find another advocate. Too much time had passed since Pierre had been sent to the Bastille. He could be dead. Athos's letters to Grignan, now a useless stack on his desk, had urged their one ally to help the young man, by faith or by foul.

Over the winter, he and Nicole plotted endlessly about Pierre, and no better plan had emerged than to recruit Grignan. Self-indulgently, Athos had been too swept up in his love for Nicole to leave her. After her husband's death, Nicole had allowed Athos inside her world. Consummating their new union had whitewashed reality. Except that Pierre ate away at her conscience. The Bastille treated men more cruelly than Hades.

While they awaited word, Athos had persuaded Nicole that Grignan was just a horrible letter-writer—a good priest, but a shamefully bad correspondent. Faced with the truth, that the letters hadn't even been opened, he sat fingering the stack on his desk and blaming himself.

A creak at his door startled him. "Don't ask me why I kept them," his landlady said. "Thought you drank most of your money, but you always found a way to pay me."

She laid a second stack of letters on the desk. Knotted in ratty twine, the bundle easily came apart.

Several came from d'Artagnan, off fighting the conflict near Prague that Athos had been excused from. Another from Tréville. And an unmarked letter laid on the bottom. Slicing it open with his knife, the flamboyant signature of Geneviève de Montpensier took up half the page. The dead Comte's mistress. Athos read the letter once, before it fluttered to the floorboards, flung aside on the way to the Vieux de Lumière, where the spider awaited the fly.

∞∞∞∞

There was no way to count the hours inside the Bastille. No sunlight of any kind illuminated the killing chambers. Pierre could count to about one hundred, so he counted to himself until the hunchback returned. Counting helped him calculate.

Somewhere around twenty-five rounds, a light flickered and the familiar dash-thump could faintly be heard. A long dash and a thump. A long dash and a thump. Pierre had never known the hunchback to speak to anyone. He'd tried at first to find out his story, something, anything, to gain a sympathetic audience. Maybe he was deaf and dumb. Not a chirp ever escaped the deformed bread-bearer.

Pierre suspected his captors were shorting his rations, as well. A week before the scalding, the intervals between feedings seemed to grow longer and longer. He wasn't sure if it was because he was giving up hope or whether they were trying to starve him. His raggedy clothes hung on him like a puppet. Without light, there was no sure way to clock his mealtime. As if a hunk of moldy bread constituted a meal.

Dash-thump.

Dash-thump.

Pierre's temples throbbed, and his scalded hand felt like it'd been placed in a spit. Both hands were above his head, like always, in order to dupe the pigeon. The key to the shackles he'd knotted to the tie on his pants.

Dash-thump.

The hunchback hobbled into the vicinity. He wore the robes of a monk, but they were so tattered and soiled no one would have believed him to be a holy man. The bump on his back caused the hem to hang unevenly. A burlap satchel held the stash of bread.

"You're coming later and later," Pierre accused, rattling his chains. "They must have convinced you we're hopeless, well, it'll be you next in here!"

As expected, it didn't faze him. Nothing ever stopped the servant from his duties. Pierre could have spit in his face—already tried—or kicked his shin—also a loss—but the deformed man went through the motions. First, the digging in his robes for the keys, then the slow sorting of one key on the ring from the next, then the approach. The hunchback held the key as if it were a sword, straight forward and away from his body. Finally, he initiated an authoritative poke of Pierre's chest. Like always.

This time, instead of succumbing to futility, Pierre slipped his hands loose of their irons and lunged directly for the man's throat. The hunchback's eyes bulged upon Pierre's tightening grip. He pushed his thumbs in just long enough for the air to cut off. A count of forty, an agonizing eternity for his burned hand, before the bread bag and its bearer dropped to the ground.

A few gasps were the extent of the struggle. Pierre's confidence increased by the width of an ocean, because it meant the hunchback probably couldn't speak and cry foul once he found himself chained to the loathsome wall.

Scrambling to change into the downed man's cloak, his weakness became apparent. Out of breath, trembling, and parched, Pierre's body dragged. The months of immobility sapped his strength. He fumbled to pull the robe from the underside of the heavy man. Unable to find footing, he tugged for longer than he should. Finally, the robe came free. Chaining the hunchback up was impossible, so he left him in a puddle instead.

Stuffing several handfuls of straw on his shoulder, Pierre prepped a disguise. Hooded, he just needed to look passable. The worst part was that he was far too skinny beneath the robes. He quickly filled his baggy pants with the last of the straw and slipped the satchel over his low shoulder. It would have to do.

In the cramped area, he practiced the limp a few times. That was the easy part. The rest would be luck and incompetence on the part of the Bastille brutes. If the hunchback was any indicator, the rest couldn't be all that sharp.

∞∞∞∞

Nicole wandered to the willow. It became her unconscious habit. The mid-morning sun or perhaps the way the birds sang caused her homing instinct to direct her to the pond and the enormous tree she loved.

So many memories were cradled in the branches. She didn't believe in spirits or ghosts. Her religion derided the supernatural. But she felt a presence under the tree. Several. She could hear the snippets of conversations between her and her sister, before their lives knotted into thorns.

"Oh, Nicole, how will you love the man you love?" Sibonne always had a way of making a simple thought complicated.

"Do you mean, how devoted will I be to him?"

"No. And yes." Sibonne giggled. "Have you kissed one yet?"

"You know the answer to that." Nicole, being the older sister, was supposed to have experienced everything first. But things were changing.

"If I tell you a secret, will you promise not even to write it in your journal?"

Nicole sighed. She never liked promising her sister anything because their pacts tended to give Sibonne the upper hand. "I suppose, but I won't tell you a secret in return." Not that she had any of the romantic kind.

"A young man in the village has been sending me love letters." Sibonne sucked in her cheeks.

Nicole's neck coloured. "There aren't any suitable men in our village … Sibonne, you know this isn't—"

"Oh, shush!" She folded her arms across her chest.

Nicole grabbed her by both elbows. The wind flung a hanging branch into her face. "Sibonne!"

"I didn't make the tree slap you! See, even the willow thinks you need to be happy for me."

"Who in the world is sending you these inappropriate letters?"

"How do you know they are inappropriate?"

"Knowing you …"

"Oh, please. Don't you want to hear one?"

"Absolutely not. You need to send Papa into town and return them with a stern message that no more notes are welcome."

Sibonne pulled one from her cleavage. Nicole fumed.

"It says," as she unfolded the creases, "that my features rival the tulip boxes in full bloom."

Simple man, simple message. Nicole wasn't impressed.

"And, that if I'm as vibrant as the tulip, I will meet him for a stroll when the moon is full."

Nicole snatched the letter with a snap. Scanning the contents, she let out an audible sigh. "It says no such thing. Sibonne, you think your little antics will force me to get on with some form of matrimony, but I won't be bullied."

"No, no, no, my sweet elder," Sibonne says, masking a faint twitter. "But Remi *has* sent me a poem, so there."

A branch rustled past Nicole's eyesight, chasing away the scene from years ago, before she had married the Comte, before her sister took her life. Her sister still confounded her. How could she have lost such hope to give up living? She missed her. Much like she missed Athos.

Other branches flapped behind her, and she assumed the wind had picked up. But the rustle turned into footsteps, and when she looked back, another vision from the past slammed into her.

∞∞∞∞

Athos found the house in the Vieux de Lumière easily. It nestled in the most upper tier of the city. Only the most wealthy, the most connected, and he feared, the most conniving, could find living quarters in this section of Paris.

Knocking on the ornate, gold-laminated door, he took a quick check of himself. Clean enough. Unshaved but that was typical, and his occasional bath had been recent. If what she had said in her letter were true, he needed to see the mistress of the Comte de Rochefort without further ado.

A servant escorted him to a parlour. The velvet on the furniture matched what he had last seen in the Queen's chamber. Fashion trends even extended to households.

The doors drew open and a slender regal woman swooshed inside then came to a standstill. Like most of the nobles in Court, her condescension followed her in, too. Geneviève de Montpensier relished her handsomeness and nobility. Coal black hair and tall, she was the human equivalent of a swan—fine lines, proud, and easily agitated. He bowed.

"Monsieur Athos," she finally said. "I expected you sooner."

He nodded. "You'll forgive me, but I came as soon as I read your letter. I've been away."

"Yes," she said and began circling the room, more or less a disguise for circling him. Her gaze never left his. "You've been in Rochefort. With your lover."

Athos bit his tongue. This was the elite of the elite. Playing their games required measured one-upsmanship. "And you, I take it, have been alone."

She immediately stopped. "The Comte's death is a permanent shadow."

"Yet you write to tell me you can help me free the man who killed him."

"A *boy*, not a *man*, monsieur. A *boy* who killed him. Pierre Tremon should perish in the Bastille."

"So you can understand my confusion about your letter."

"It brings you here." Geneviève's grim frown changed into a snide smile. "I find, monsieur, that the most pure of heart can often be duped. You and your earnest friends think truth and honesty will win the day. Very little in my experience supports that thinking."

Athos kept his face still.

"Let's start with what we know," she continued. "The Comte de Rochefort's nephew killed my lover. François loved me, no matter what you may think. For his death, I want retribution."

"But Pierre may be dead already. The Bastille is retribution multiplied by an eternity."

"Not to me it isn't. I want to see him suffer, *cause* his suffering. And so does Vachon."

"Vachon?" Athos couldn't fathom how the two knew each other, let alone devise a plan.

"He's even more blood-thirsty than I am," Geneviève said. "Henri's death tore him apart."

Athos couldn't believe Pierre's bad luck. Not one, but two ruthless enemies wanted to cut off his head. He wished he had more time to think. "No one's answered my requests to release him from the Bastille or to grant me access to see him. I have nothing to offer you."

"Ah, monsieur. You have everything to offer me. Because you care too much about him. It's the sole reason you even returned to Paris. Or shall I say, it was the only reason Nicole sent you. It's her, really, that you care so much about."

"She's no one to you."

"But she's everything to you." Geneviève moved toward him, across the rug, an act that seemed to stop time. Athos felt the next tick would drop like a bomb. "She's the most important thing to you, and that is why I have taken her."

For an instant, the statement exploded between his ears. "Don't play with me."

Geneviève slid a foot or two closer. Her eyes widened. "I have her, your one true love. That's it, isn't it? She's the one. The only person you'd give up your life for. Relinquish your duty to the King."

Forgoing restraint, Athos bounded forward and grabbed her hand. "You beast!"

She jerked her hand away and produced a fan from her pocket. She flapped it open.

"If you don't cooperate, I dare say Vachon will choose to reap his vengeance on her rather than Pierre."

"I wouldn't make such threats," he said, swatting the fan down to the ground. "There's more to the rumours about my ruthlessness than you know."

She backed up and headed for the desk. From it, she picked up a note.

"I have here a note from the Cardinal," she started.

Richelieu? Athos thought his ears were playing tricks. But given the nature of the circumstances, nothing seemed truly impossible.

"This note absolves the bearer of any criminal act," she continued. "I offer you this in exchange for Pierre, should you pluck him from the Bastille. Once I have him, Nicole will be freed."

Athos tromped across the room and tried to snatch the note from her. She dodged to the opposite side of a loveseat.

"You won't overtake me, Monsieur. I'm the only one who knows of Vachon's whereabouts with Nicole. If you're smart, you'll heed me. Free Pierre, by any means possible, and be absolved of it. Once he's in my possession, I shall release your one true love."

The whites in Athos's eyes might as well have turned red. "I'll be beholden to no one!"

"Oh, but you will. Once you relent, nothing will block your way," she said, ending with a small sigh. "Yes, Monsieur Athos, I have studied you. And everyone, from the lowliest peasant to the King, says you are a single-minded individual and will accomplish the impossible if determined to do so. I have no qualms about you. I hold the ultimate card."

He'd miscalculated her ruthlessness. In his rage, he could have sliced her tongue out.

"I'll give you three days," she said and turned to leave. At the sliding parlour doors, she looked over her shoulder and hummed a little to herself. "I see what everyone says about you."

He stared sternly at her.

"Not a man in Paris is your rival."

At the clap of the door, Athos pounded the desk and toppled a servant on his way out.

∞∞∞

The cells in the Bastille stacked end-to-end, and Pierre emptied the bread satchel much sooner than he anticipated. Each new turn in the cavernous killing ground took him to another corner of suffering. He saw things that he might never erase from memory. Amputees, blinded men, mouths sewn shut. Scalding had been a warm-up, he realized. Bones, perhaps ribs, littered the dirt floor, a few with flesh still attached. He held back the bile because the hunchback would have seen this all before. The carnage. The flat-out disregard for human life. It was ironic that food of any sort was offered these creatures, stripped of their humanity, dignity, any fragment of normalcy.

At the end of his rounds, or what he thought to be the end, he came to a locked barricade. A heavy door with a barred window stood between him and what? An exit? Another round of putrid deliveries? He knocked a few times with the back of his hand, soft but not lacking confidence.

A brute with a patch over one eye peered through the bars. Pierre tucked his chin tighter to his chest, afraid the man might get a glimpse under his hood.

"Secret word?"

The one-eyed gatekeeper said it like he'd repeated the question a thousand times. Probably had. The fatigue in the voice conveyed a familiar attitude. Anyone who had bothered to shout or talk to him in here didn't care.

One or two seconds passed, and Pierre mentally ticked off one guess after another searching for the right phrase. Then it dawned on him. If the hunchback was truly mute, he would never be expected to say a thing. He simply knocked again.

The single eye blinked and disappeared. A few seconds passed before a key turned, and the iron latch clanged open in the echo chamber. The man stepped aside and patted the satchel as Pierre walked past.

"Hunk of bread?" he said.

Pierre shook his head.

"You idiot." There was a distinct irritation in the guard's comeback, but a familiar one, like these scenes had unfolded a thousand times before, and tonight, or today, was just the same.

∞∞∞

Athos ran down the streets of Paris and ended at the Musketeer base, often called the House of Trèville. The headquarters run by Monsieur de Trèville never looked so inviting. To shore up, there was no better place than among the King's finest men—his Musketeers.

He hadn't come with a purpose other than to shake off the deleterious encounter with the Comte's lover. Swords clanged robustly in the main room where several practiced. The sound covered him in a familiar salve. In his time as a King's servant, nothing had prepared him for going head-to-head with a murderous aristocrat. More specifically, a murderous madame.

Except for Milady. She had been in a class by herself. Milady's passionate but violent nature fed her every decision. But like Milady, Geneviève sought vengeance. Women filled with hate defied conventional tactics. Seeing his brethren in the House of Trèville, Athos arrived at a plan. He had but one choice, free Pierre for his own sake, and take the chance that once free, the hateful woman would focus on the true culprit.

He had precious little time to implement his strategy. Once Pierre was free, Athos's greatest need would be to find Nicole and take her home. His window of opportunity would be infinitesimally small.

"Athos? Is that you?"

Athos turned to find a familiar face. Camille's.

He grabbed the fellow's hand and shook it vigorously then gave him an uncharacteristic hug.

"All right, I see you appreciate an old friend," Camille said, laughing between squeezes.

"My God, I can't believe you're here in one piece!"

"Trust me, I'm as good as new." Camille crowed like a rooster. Several in the vicinity crowed back.

Athos beamed. "You had me worried back with the gypsies. I see they did you no harm."

"They were a fine lot to leave me with. They might have their peculiarities, but they couldn't stand to see a man die whom they held nothing against." Camille swiveled this way and that, demonstrating that his essential parts worked properly.

"And how in the devil did you end up here?"

"Isn't that obvious?" Camille's forehead screwed up. "You killed my boss. I needed a job."

"You mean, Pierre killed him."

"Well, you were in the midst of all that insanity, defending your one and only."

"I shall never live it down."

"And why should you? It's a fabulous story."

Athos shook Camille's shoulder good-naturedly, still flabbergasted by the discovery of his friend again. His respect for Camille matched that of his long-time compatriots, Aramis and Porthos, who'd left the King's service for quieter lives. "You show up back in my life at a very good time."

"Oh no! I hear an intrigue brewing."

"It's worse," Athos said and pulled Camille under the stairwell into a quieter nook. "So much worse I can scarcely grapple with it."

"And what say you? How can I help?"

Athos took precious little time describing the turn of events. Given Camille's understanding of the travails leading up to the present, Athos counted on him to fill in the necessary blanks and surmise that the intrigue had only resumed.

"My God," Camille whispered, rubbing the back of his neck. "And how will you find Nicole? Do you have any idea where she might be hidden?"

"I do. It will require sending out spies to every convent and monastery close to Paris. They can't be keeping her too far away. Vachon would want to be close to Paris once Pierre is handed over. If he's as blood-thirsty as Geneviève would have me believe, he'll want Pierre's hide on a spit within hours, not days."

"So, where do we start?"

Camille's willingness revived Athos's hope. When it came to Nicole, he often found hope was the singular thread that tied them together. He had to put the inconceivable aside—that he might lose her, lose his son, lose all the good that God had placed in his hands. Displacing his worry, he stepped into the gallery and shouted above the fray.

"Ho! My fellow Musketeers!"

The clamour inside the room stilled. Whispered conversations filtered through the space.

"As one among you, I come seeking assistance. I need to locate a captive, and you can help."

Nods and smiles quickly spread. One guardsman called, "Anything for the legendary Athos."

Taking little of it to his head, he declared, "Then gather here, I need you all. All for one and one for all."

∞∞∞∞

Though he'd gotten through the first checkpoint, Pierre held no clues to the next one, if there were a next one. The Bastille's tricky labyrinth confused him. The passageways twisted in illogical patterns and turned into dead ends and blank walls. Sweat ran down his back and legs beneath the hunchback's robes. His aches and burns needled his resolve. His physical condition crumbled his hope of ever finding a way out.

He wandered into a section that seemed far emptier than the one he had been imprisoned in, so his intuition told him he must be on the right track. If there were layers to Hell, he was one rosary bead above awful.

Several men were chained to walls as he had been. He worried if he crisscrossed in confusion that their suspicion would be aroused, and they'd call him out. But nothing seemed to faze the men. They languished as he had, dull to hope.

A rat raced by an opening he had not yet taken, and he decided if anyone, or anything, might know these passages well, it was the creature that contributed to its destitution.

The rat sniffed along the path and didn't flinch as Pierre trailed him. A new smell began to come from ahead, that of burning torches. This meant better conditions and possibly another checkpoint to finagle his way past.

The murmurs of a clipped conversation drifted toward him as Pierre slowed to a near-crawl. He wanted to hear the exchange first before he initiated the next phase of his escape.

"They're gathering the able-bodied now. Any man who can stand and hold a spike goes," a wheezy voice said. A fit of coughing ensued.

"Last rites are important then," responded a familiar voice. "You've denied these lost souls every dignity known to man, but you should not deny them the dignity of salvation."

Pierre knew the voice. The cadence and pitch gave him away. It was the priest who had given him the apple. The man spoke as if he had one ear to God's mouth and a fist clenched in defiance, but only slightly.

Pierre's heartbeat doubled. Maybe God was giving him the ultimate chance for escape. He decided to wait out the continuing argument. If the priest got inside, there was a possibility for a cleaner getaway.

The wheezy guardsman sparred verbally with the priest for several minutes. If he even was a priest. Maybe he was in disguise, just as Pierre was, striving for believability. Whatever the case, the priest had handed Pierre the keys to freedom, and he needed him again to climb to safety.

"Come back 'morrow, old man," the wheezer said. "They'll drag the lucky off in batches. The carts will be lopsided and you can pray 'em free then."

"Lucky?" the priest asked, frustration in his tone. "No man forced into battle deserves such luck."

"Better than 'ere."

Pierre heard what sounded like the men parting ways, feet shuffling, objects dragging, and he built up his resolve. Using his practiced limp, he pulled himself into the opening. The torchlight caused his eyes to burn and water. It was the most light he'd seen since he'd been bound to foul fortunes.

"Ah, a kindred spirit." The priest pivoted toward Pierre, who just kept walking, unsure how to give the man a signal. He just wanted out. Ignoring the man's pleasantries would be a small price—but the clergyman probably was there because of him. Or maybe a dozen others he wanted to set free.

The second Pierre came within grabbing distance, he thrust the satchel toward the priest, and although taken aback, he took the bait. Pierre didn't stop walking. Drag-thump. He tottered forward, lurching toward the way out, pulling his new companion.

"I have nothing for your … uh … offering." But the priest didn't let go.

"See, even the lackey knows yer better off gone." The guard took a torch off its perch. "Don't forget this."

The light might as well been the keys to the castle. Feeling his luck had finally returned, Pierre limped toward a staircase ahead in the long narrowing hall. Up and out.

∞∞∞∞

Athos devised a plan more sophisticated than the most tactical wartime maneuvers. Musketeers in groups of three would infiltrate the convents in the surrounding countryside from Le Mans to Lure in east and west quadrants and Cambrai and Bourges in north and south. The most junior of the Musketeers, men with less than a year in the company, were assigned the four monasteries. Those compounds would be easier to enter and search.

Nicole wouldn't necessarily be hiding in plain sight, he told his allies. Describing Vachon, Athos warned the men their nemesis would be lethal and merciless.

"It's likely he's bribed the most important people where you'll go, and their secrecy will be bound by the threat of retaliation. If Vachon's and Nicole's whereabouts are revealed," Athos said, swiping his hand over a map of central France, "it could mean many lives will be in danger."

"He can't be much of a swordsman if none of us have ever heard of him," a young Musketeer said, inducing a round of back slaps and *ayes* from the circle around the large table.

Camille interjected. "He's spent his life under the tutelage of the Comte de Rochefort. As you know of his demise," a glance to Athos, "his skill was never in question."

"My only reluctance is that I cannot go with you," Athos said. "Pierre is who Vachon really wants, and if he's free, Nicole is of lesser value to him. Unfortunately, the Bastille will be the equivalent of breaking into a fortress."

Athos widened the circle of men and ended his instruction bearing even grimmer news.

"One last thing," he said, saving the most important for last, "Nicole is with child."

# 4

# The Captive

Over a mind-bending forty-eight hours, Nicole's energy evaporated. Her back ached from the strain of the long carriage ride. In charge on horseback, her kidnapper stalked his captive as they fled to a point unknown. It was not so much Nicole's intuition as his grave intensity that told her a river of hatred fueled the fire. Again, she was locked inside the vestige of a previous life.

At dusk, they arrived at Avrillé, a small town on the outskirts of Angers. As she came off the coach, he finally revealed to her why he looked so familiar.

"My brother was Henri. You're the reason he's dead."

Now she remembered. Vachon had been an underling of her husband's.

Inside the inn where he locked her for the night, she crumpled into the sagging middle of the bed. The night of Henri's murder came tumbling back. The chase from Le Mans.

The surging threat of the horseman. Henri's unwanted kisses. And then the blood. And Pierre, reaping the spoils of killing a man. Killing Vachon's only brother.

Now, she paid a heavy toll.

Her clothes, soiled from the kidnapping, felt strangling. She toiled to loosen them at a basin of cool water. There was no mirror in the shabby inn. A blessing for her. Her suffering deserved to be hidden from the eyes of everyone, including herself.

She curled on the bed and hugged her middle. The baby hadn't moved 'much during the carriage ride. Probably the rocking lulled the child to sleep. She wished the same for herself. Sleep induced such fanciful notions of serenity. Her love of Athos always seemed to come with a thread of disharmony. Another level of strain. Would they ever be free of it?

She was awakened from sleep by Vachon aggressively shaking her shoulder. He smelled of wine.

"What kind of woman are you?" His tongue struggled to form the vowels. "Wealth, privilege, yet you throw it away. For a wayward soldier of the King? You fool." He hiccupped. "Men like him, like me, only live and breathe by the sword."

Vachon leaned closer, his eyes jerking to stay focused on the hair down her back. "I see what he sees. You have those qualities," hiccup, "that of an Aphrodite." He petted a thick lock and whiffed the curled end. "I have you instead of him."

Nicole strained against another touch, but Vachon fumbled to his feet and fell, bottom down, on the floor. He attempted to laugh but his drunkenness thickened his voice to unrecognizable.

"Why do you want me? I'm a pariah."

"You're the cheese," he pronounced, an extra long *ee*.

"The what?"

"The morsel we'll use to lure your lover into a trap." Vachon, though drunk, slapped his hands together with a resounding sharpness. "Once we have him and Pierre, then the real fun begins."

Nicole didn't know what to believe. She understood the undertow of revenge. She often blamed her husband for her life's travails. As his widow, she'd fallen to pawn status. She was simply a pawn.

"Let me go."

Vachon snatched a glimpse over his shoulder. "You're more valuable than my sword."

"Let me go," she said and raised herself up. "I'm with child. I have vast stores of wealth. Take any amount of it you want. There's only one thing here worth saving." She placed a hand on her wide belly.

Vachon's stomach couldn't decide whether to gurgle or hiccup or chuckle. After an extended intestinal tug-of-war, he sighed.

"Comtesse," he faked a bow from sitting. "It's my distinct pleasure to introduce you to the world of intrigue. You, Madame, are no longer a bystander. You are the centrepointe itself."

Vachon promptly passed out.

Nicole dropped back into the bed, partly wanting to run, partly wanting to cry. Her head jumbled over which way out.

Even before Vachon had said so, she suspected she was kidnapped because of the trouble she'd stirred. Not that she bore the entire responsibility for her nephew's actions. Pierre had only been trying to defend her from her husband's henchmen when he killed Henri.

But her current circumstances cut a deep line through her store of courage. Athos would come for her, as certain as the sun would rise. The stakes were so high that nothing would stop him.

Nicole stared down at the snoozing culprit. She slipped off the bed and nudged him with a toe when she was convinced he was too far gone.

Slowly, cautiously, she prepared herself to take up her own cause. Recalibrating her thoughts, she left the cottage and made her way to the only place that provided the safety she needed.

∞∞∞

Four steps from the top of the staircase, Pierre pulled the hood off his disguise. The priest nodded in affirmation. "I realized it was you because of this." Taking Pierre's scalded hand, he said a short prayer.

"It's as Monsieur Athos told me it would be," the young man said.

The priest shook his head in misunderstanding.

"The pain," Pierre told him. He gently returned his injured hands beneath the robes. "Once you get used to it, you become numb."

"I can't imagine."

"Who are you?" Pierre's incredulity was difficult to mask. He wanted to feel grateful, but at the same time his frustration due to the long imprisonment condensed his gratitude into a tight ball.

"I'm Simon Grignan. Father Grignan. A friend of friends."

"The priest who gave Nicole sanctuary."

"The very one."

Pierre took the next few steps cautiously. "Where does this lead, Simon Grignan?" He couldn't resist a dollop of sarcasm.

"Another checkpoint, down another corridor. More stairs and guards. But your disguise should work."

"Until the real hunchback wakes up."

"Well, there never is a foolproof plan, so we hurry."

Grignan took the lead. Pierre stopped pretending to limp to make time. The level they had come to was less of a Hell hole, if that was possible. A few more torches filled the winding passageways and fewer men seemed to be moaning.

"Was I on the bottom rung?" Pierre almost didn't want to know.

"Had you been any lower, you would not have been of this world."

Pierre held back a hard swallow and kept moving. Soon the two heard voices. Grignan stretched out an arm to stop him and mimicked he would do the talking.

Three guards stuck to their huddle. They eyeballed something at their feet. A dice game.

The priest cleared his throat, and one of the brutes glanced over. He grunted and returned to their game.

Pierre put his limp back into play and dragged behind Grignan. Before he could get past the men, one of them grabbed him by the arm.

"You, hunchback," the grizzled man said, almost grunted. "Everyone says you're mute."

The man by his side elbowed him in the ribs. "Your turn."

"Let's bet the hunchy is faking it," the first man said, tightening his grip on Pierre's upper arm. He squirmed a little before Grignan stepped in.

"I assure you my good men," the priest said and rested a hand on the assaulting guard's shoulder, "this unfortunate creature is as voiceless as the wind."

"I dunno," the third blurted, "the wind kept me awake hollowing three nights ago."

All the guards chortled. The first held tightly to Pierre.

"I have an idea," he said. "If he squeals, we throw him in the rat pool. If he keeps his tongue, I'll buy us all a round at sunrise."

A dread covered the next beat of silence. The second guard scooped the dice from the floor. "What'll you do? Punch him."

"Better," the offending gambler said. "See if my reflexes are still good."

The guard pulled a knife from his back belt and pulled Pierre toward a small stump of wood that acted as a makeshift table. A sheen on the top resembled sticky blood.

The man slapped one hand on the stump. He stuck the knife between each finger, slowly, to demonstrate. "Of course, I can go much faster."

The other two guards sounded off nervous laughs.

"You," the guard said, jamming the blunt end of the knife into Pierre's waist. The hay inside his pants padded the impact. "Hand down."

He shook his head. Grignan tried again to de-escalate. "This man suffers daily the travails of deformity and the terrible conditions of this place. Leave him be. My time is limited for this useless nonsense."

The guard acted as if the priest were invisible. He manhandled Pierre to kneeling and jerked one of his hands from his robe.

The instant it slammed the stump, Pierre's every nerve screamed.

"Well, look at this," the guard said and pointed with the knife. "What have we here?"

"Looks like he's been in the scalding room," the second teetered.

"None of us are immune to the nature of this place," Grignan said. He tried stepping in-between the guard and Pierre, but the guard wouldn't have it. He brushed him to the side with a hard swipe.

"Not making your deliveries on time? Napping on duty? Guess we'll never know," the guard said and flashed his knife. "Then this won't seem so terrible."

Pierre instinctively spread his fingers as wide as possible. The skin between his finger joints seared in pain. Maybe the scald could mask a near-miss. Could there be any greater pain than what he was experiencing now?

The guard plunked the blade from space to space, moving at a slow, rhythmic pace. All eyes were trained on the knife. The thunk of the blade in the wood and its subsequent twang upon release reminded Pierre of shooting a bow. Ironically, he could never get his aim right.

The poking sped up. The guard sucked air through his teeth and released little bursts after five or so stabs. The real trick was finessing the depth of the blade in the stump so that the release and next prick didn't snag the rhythm. Pierre noticed a tiny line of sweat trickle down the guard's temple.

One small squeak from Pierre could ruin him.

The second guard jostled the third, both smiling. "I'll bet my week's wages you'll miss."

He went faster. In flashes of dull iron, the blade jumped between Pierre's fingers. Then the game ended.

The blade struck deep and severed the end of Pierre's pinkie. A riptide of agony raced up his spine, but he bit his tongue, literally, until it bled. Not a foul word escaped him. The end of his finger lay like detritus, and blood covered the nub. Blinking rapidly, Pierre dropped to the ground.

He had no knowledge how long it took him to come to. When he did, Grignan sat next to him, also shackled.

"They didn't believe a word of it." He meant the feigned excuses. Pierre knew what he meant.

Pierre had been stripped of his robe and the straw. What was left was his skeletal frame, filthy clothes, and a finger wrapped tightly with a short scrap of twine. It had stopped bleeding. It had not stopped throbbing.

Pierre flopped his head toward Grignan, whose eyes scanned this way and that. They were in a room he couldn't remember having been in. But the place was always so dark and unwelcoming, nothing left much of an impression.

"We're being sent to fight. France is fighting against the Protestants near Prague. All capable men are fodder for recruits, even criminals." Grignan turned his eyes on Pierre. "Are you going to be all right?"

Pierre failed to process the question or form an answer.

"You never uttered a word," Grignan said, a little on the side of astonishment. "How?"

Again, no answer. Instead, Pierre leaned to one side and dry-heaved. Saliva dribbled down his chin, but his tongue was too swollen to attempt much help.

"Rest," Grignan tried to reassure. "Where they're sending us, we'll need it."

∞ ∞ ∞

Nicole thanked God for making His places of worship the largest and most central part of French villages. She found one in Avrillé within a short distance of the cottage.

In the middle of the night, knocking seemed pointless. The front doors were locked and the heavy iron pulls felt familiar and a little cold. She prayed they would open like the sea for Moses. But that selfish thought forced her to step back and form a different plan.

A high stone wall surrounded the back of the church. Obviously, quarters for monks or nuns or both lay on the opposite side. She quickly circled the perimeter until she found an iron gate. The latch, also locked, nested in place loosely. It had enough play that she could rattle it. Maybe a light sleeper, a sympathetic ear, would arouse and let her in. It was all she had to hope for.

She didn't want to call out because she feared the neighbourhood would hear the sounds of a woman in distress. Vachon might have an easier time tracking her if a willing villager supplied an eye-witness account for a few coins.

She rattled and paused. Rattled and paused. The minutes turned into darker prospects. A cool wind on her neck caused goosebumps. Her stomach ached in hunger. Vachon, while quick to fill his empty belly with wine, hadn't offered her a speck of food. Her rattles grew more desperate.

A tiny rustle, almost the sound of a mouse at a pantry door, caused her to stop. Something stirred on the good side of the gate, enough of a sound that she pressed her cheeks to the iron, hoping to catch a glimpse in the dark. From the night arose a soft-spoken voice.

"Who goes there?" a woman's voice called from far away in the stillness.

"Please, I'm in need of sanctuary." Nicole shivered from another cool wind on her neck.

A short shadow crept into her view. A figure soon became visible, petite and a little bent forward. The woman wasn't in a rush to decide her fate.

"I'm not from this village," Nicole said. "I've been brought here by circumstances beyond my control, and I need a place to stay, at least for a night." She didn't mean to, but the gate rattled again under her intense desire to get on the other side.

"What's your name?" The voice had the qualities of old age, a gravelly drag.

"Nicole Rieux, the Comtesse de Rochefort."

"The Comtesse de Rochefort?"

Nicole hesitated. "Far from home."

The woman appeared at the lock almost instantly, and her granny hands unlatched the gate and opened it just enough for her to slip through. In a warm feather-light grasp, Nicole held her benefactor's hand and stayed as close to the woman's back as possible without tripping on her heels. The woman rounded a few turns and guided her toward a black box structure. A creaky handle introduced them to a small room that finally cast light on the tiny stranger.

The woman was shrunken by age. Her serious eyes, though kind, gave Nicole a thorough assessment. Eyes never age, thought Nicole. This woman's pair had seen more than its share of bumps in the night.

"Thank you," Nicole said before letting the woman's hand go.

"Hmm." Her head titled to one side, and she sighed after one look at Nicole's belly.

Self-consciously, Nicole wrapped her arms around herself and sighed back.

"We don't receive many people," the woman said, "but here, sit."

"Isn't this a place of God?"

"Hmm, in a way." The woman busied herself behind Nicole at a two-shelf cupboard and square counter braced to the wall. The room, varying shades of brown, included a pallet, a stool, and a wash basin on a pedestal. A small wood stove took up a corner. The embers from a recent fire were more black than red. A stubby candle burned in a pewter candlestick.

"You live here," Nicole stated rather than questioned, simply a fact.

"And you don't," the woman said.

She didn't take offense. "May I ask your name?"

The woman came around and presented a mug of milk within Nicole's reach. She took it and nodded thanks.

"Odile. Once a nun, always a nun."

"Then this is a convent?"

"No, no. Not in many years. I'm the caretaker. No one but me and the priest, if you want to call him that."

Nicole's expression relayed her confusion.

"He drinks too much."

Not even clergy were immune to the temptation of spirits. Nicole sipped her milk and inhaled its fresh goodness.

"And why are you here? Knocking in the night?" Odile stooped low to sit on the stool. It made her look even more diminutive and frail. She was as old as any person Nicole had memory of, and it amazed her that God continued to grant the gift of time.

"My life tends toward the complicated."

"Hmm, I see," Odile said, another eye on Nicole's middle. "When will the baby come?"

"Not for a while." Nicole took another drink.

"You don't look entirely like a lost damsel, but my judgment somewhat went out with the parishioners."

"Are you alone here, as you say?"

"Most days. There's a gardener who tends the vegetables. Hmm, might be sorry for us."

Nicole cast a half smile. "What happened to the church?"

"Behind on taxes. Drank up, my dear. I showed up before the worst, then got too old to go out with the rest."

"Somewhere there must be a blessing for your continued occupation here."

"Hmm." Odile adjusted the long brown skirt to smooth a wrinkle over her bony knees. The skirt hem was frayed all the way around.

Nicole decided it was safe to be more forthcoming. "I need to remain hidden. A man in the village brought me here against my will. I need to wait until he's gone before I can feel safe to leave. I believe he will leave tomorrow if he doesn't find me. He may look here because it's obvious. Would you, could you …?"

"Hard to believe a woman of your stature is on the run." Odile scratched a shin with her ribbed fingernails. "This man, is he the Comte? Your husband?"

Nicole gulped. "No."

Odile raised an eyebrow. "A relative?"

Nicole shook her head.

"Dastardly, I see." Under her skirt and beneath the stool, Odile patted the floor in search of something. Once she found what she was looking for, she showed the cover to Nicole. It was a book of devotionals, tooled in leather with the title *Meditations of the Ursalines.*

Nicole tried reading the woman's expression. "Are you …?"

"Am I what?"

"An Ursaline?"

"Once. Now just a caretaker."

"I know of them. A priest in Paris, a dear friend of mine, informed me of your existence."

"Oh, we exist. Or did. My order is long gone."

"But not in spirit." Nicole reached out to see if the nun would hand over the book. Odile obliged.

In Nicole's hand, the book transferred the feeling of great importance. Her prior reading about the order's liberal beliefs, which had come from Father Grignan, made her want to know more. Ironically, the opportunity came at an inopportune time.

"What if he doesn't leave?" Odile's mouth scrunched into a small pucker.

Nicole squeezed the book tighter. "I won't lie. He may use force."

"Hmm."

"I'd understand if you decide to send me away."

"God strike me down if I do," Odile quickly replied. She rubbed her hands together and folded them into one another. "Inside, I'll show you. At dawn. A perfect hiding place."

Nicole crossed herself, and her new elderly ally followed suit.

# 5

# Rallying for Escape

Athos and Camille spent the better part of the next morning rounding up wretches from gutters and the most detestable drinking establishments in Paris to locate any man who'd been in the depths of the Bastille. Almost to a fault, each man sober enough to have a conversation regaled them with the myths of one tale of torture after another. But none had actually been there.

That confirmed the prison's reputation—it was not a place one lived through.

By noon, a crowd stirred in the street over an event underway in the square at Notre Dame. Athos cornered a young shopkeeper to discover that Cardinal Richelieu's guards were gathering men for the conflict against the Hapsburgs. Gathering was a euphemism that meant forced recruitment. Not that this fact kept the peasants at bay. Any excuse for voyeurism in Paris drew a crowd.

But the shopkeeper also said men from the Bastille would be among the scores sent off for service. Athos and Camille immediately joined the curiosity seekers advancing toward the square.

The number of people shocked the two men. Several hundred clamoured for a view of the stage. A wooden platform, the kind used for hangings, had been erected for the occasion. Women and children held rotten chunks of cabbages, ready to pelt at the guards, at Cardinal Richelieu, or anyone unlucky enough to stand within throwing distance. Good sense never seemed to rule in the public square.

On both sides of the stage, cages on wagons held a sparse assortment of bedraggled men. From the back of the ocean of people, Athos couldn't identify any of the characters already detained. He motioned for Camille to go one way, him the other, and meet closer to the unlucky recruits. Lucky perhaps to be out of one Hell and headed for another.

A shirtless muscle man paced across the platform and banged a gong. It had the opposite effect of quieting the crowd. As he got closer, Athos could hear the thug shouting.

"Every man with one good arm for firing a weapon and two good feet to walk a mile must claim their position in the Cardinal's army." No matter, the crowd jeered and pelted the thug with garbage.

A saucy adolescent called back, "So you can cage us for war? What are we? Animals?"

Cheers made waves around the heads in the crowds.

Athos came to an opening near the front. Bumping through the wall of people, he saw one prison wagon more clearly. Most of the dozen or so men stared blankly through the rough bars into the open air. A couple snoozed. Each listless man appeared to have had the life beat out of him already. Dirty. Vacant in the eye. Curled inward. Torture had the ability to strip the most confident men of their manhood.

Camille waved from the other side of the crowd and shouted. Athos couldn't hear him above the noise.

The thug on the stage started in on his unpersuasive litany of demands and stopped mid-sentence, fixing his eyes on Athos.

"Mesdemoiselles and messieurs, if you don't believe me, then take a Musketeer's word for it." The burly announcer grabbed Athos by the collar and hoisted him onstage.

"Tell us. Tell us your stories, Musketeer, the glories of war. You look like a fighting man."

Cheers roiled up from the crowd.

Athos pulled his sword from its scabbard, not knowing whether he wanted to make a show or just get off the stage. The showman took it as a sign the new player was game.

"A swordsman extraordinaire!" The thug clanged the gong several times and marched around Athos, who suddenly felt like he'd entered the ranks of a festival troupe. "Show us how a real man takes the enemy down."

Athos paced from one end of the stage to the other, more interested in getting a better look at who was in the caged wagons than what kind of show he was going to put on. A woman in front of the stage tossed a dead rat at his feet, and he turned around and skewered the rodent and lifted it like a torch.

"See here!" He said and shook the rat. The crowd whipped into an uproar, but Athos stood so still and frowned so sternly that the applause and cheers died down. He remained still and silent until even the babies had stopped crying.

"My suffering is your suffering. Not a man among Musketeers can attest to the good of war. If you kill a man, the rest of your life is tied to death. Do not rejoice or mock the killing. Do not come to this place for entertainment. These are the men that used to be yours," he shouted and pointed back at the caged inhabitants, "that are our fathers and brothers. Men you forsake and ask no accountability of their keepers. We live in the shadow of this shame."

Several of the men in the crowd nodded. A few removed their hats.

"If I could lay my sword aside, I would." A few quiet gasps rose from women. "But until I'm safe from the darker forces of men and their greed and false desires, my sword will never leave me."

He flung the rat at the strong man who had stayed dumb throughout the whole soliloquy. Chanting began in the back of the square. It rippled through the lines of people, until it caught up to the front.

*Athos! Athos! Athos! Athos!*

Whether he liked it or not, his legend lived on.

From a corner of the stage, Camille waved frantically. Athos knelt down to him.

"The chanting did the trick," he said and shook Athos joyously by the neck. "Your man Pierre heard your name."

Athos leapt down and dodged the gropes and pulls of gregarious fans. The gonging on stage resumed. In the last wagon, chained to each other, Pierre and Simon Grignan gripped the bars in anticipatory relief.

"Pierre!" Athos grabbed his head through the bars and hid his astonishment at the young man's weakened condition. "Your hand."

Sections were peeling, redder and rawer beneath the burns. Pierre pointed to his mouth.

"Water," Athos said to Camille, and they both began shaking down nearby men. A pouch was procured.

Pouring the water as best he could through the iron into Pierre's mouth, Athos finally acknowledged Grignan. "I've been worried about you, too."

"In far less peril than many others," Grignan said, always the optimist.

Water splattered Pierre's face but he caught as much on his tongue as he could manage.

"How did you end up in there with him?" Athos asked.

"My rescue attempt backfired."

"I'm sorry I wasn't there to help."

"Well," Grignan said, trying to reach out to pat Athos but not having quite enough length on his chain, "God can have a flair for the dramatic."

In an aside, Camille said to them, "We're drawing attention."

Several guards wearing emblems of the Cardinal had climbed onstage and were peering back at the wagons. Athos had to think fast.

"There's no way we're going to get them out now," he said.

"Unless it appears we're not the ones causing the ruckus," Grignan said and moved his eyes toward the crowd. "Use them."

Athos squeezed the priest's hand and got to work.

It took less than a half-minute for him to rally a band of men to start rocking the wagon. Soon, others joined in. Athos had to give his countrymen credit. When directed in the right way, their boisterous, rowdy nature could have value.

Soon, groups of men, full of the pent-up energy from poor circumstances and mob idealism, were rocking all six wagons surrounding the stage. It was too much mayhem for the Cardinal's guards to control, though a few tried punching a couple of the most rampage-crazed men, only to be tripped or assaulted with cabbage.

Athos and Camille didn't have to direct or participate. They just waited until their wagon tipped, and their desired cargo fell safely into their arms.

∞∞∞

Nicole couldn't sleep. Odile snored lightly, huddled on the floor. The old woman had done the courtesy of giving her the lumpy bed, but it didn't bring on restfulness. She'd wished the nun had taken her to the hiding place right away rather than wait until first light.

She read as much of the devotional as she could until the short candle burned out. As she understood, the Ursalines were focused on teaching. They wanted young, old, privileged, and poor to have access to knowledge. Not only scholars could be teachers, but anyone. They advocated for ordinary men and women to pass on religious and scholarly thought and improve lives.

The prayers in the devotional struck Nicole as having the feeling of conventional religious doctrine. Similar words and rhythms filled the small book. Odile had folded the corners of pages on several passages, and lightly scribbled notes filled the margins.

*And God shall reward the meek …*

*No good tree grows without bearing fruit …*

Nicole had lived by these ideals her entire life. Why her life had veered again into wickedness wasn't answered in these pages. So, too, the broader, poignant questions about life's meaning eluded even the greatest of religious writing. Or at least she was bold enough to think they did.

Odile shook her from a light sleep when the black turned to gray outside. She offered her another cup of milk and a chunk of hard bread. Without speaking a word, the two left the nun's sparse quarters and headed toward the church.

Outside, the morning dew clung to Nicole's shoes and skirt. They walked through a neatly manicured garden toward the back entrance of the church. Up three steps and inside a heavy door, they entered what felt like a tomb to Nicole. The musty air clung to her, and the smell of old books and incense grew stronger the deeper they moved inside.

The church was much smaller than hers in Rochefort and housed only five rows of pews. The seats were covered in dust.

"Are no services held here at all?"

Odile stopped for a moment and looked the place up and down, like she hadn't in a while. "Village got tired of his slurred speech. Never had enough wine for communion." Her mouth turned down on one side, probably a memory she wanted to forget.

"Where is he?"

"Hmm. Hard to say. Sometimes he's asleep in his study. Other nights he convinces a family in the village to put him up. Only if they have wine, though."

Odile pushed on and Nicole hung back a moment to look at the altar and the rudimentary stained glass. A cross was as fanciful a design as the church displayed, but the colorful light shone in and lightened her mood by a fraction.

Her feet had swollen during the carriage ride, and they hadn't gotten better. The baby seemed to like the bumpy ride but now he was kicking.

"Here," Odile's voice came from an alcove.

Nicole found Odile standing next to the confessional.

"Isn't that an obvious place to hide a runaway?"

"Hmm. Never thought of it." Odile opened the door. "But this one is special."

Odile had Nicole come closer and showed her that a plank on one side of the booth opened a thin door into another compartment. Room enough for one, if the one didn't mind being cramped. No wonder Odile hadn't been in a hurry last night.

"See here," Odile said, pushing on a wood lever inside the hidden cell that released a spring lock. "If inside, you press this and out you pop."

Nicole stuck her head in and checked the size. A few cobwebs stuck to her face. Her head could swivel but her body, especially her belly, would be wedged in tight. "It's so small. Who in the world would need such a place?"

"Someone who liked to get an earful," Odile said, one eye twinkling.

"How did you find it?"

"Priest showed me."

"Does he check it before he hears confessions?"

"Don't know. If he did, that would have been years ago."

Years. Nicole sympathized with the faithful who may have been denied a good religious home. How could the church turn such a blind eye to their needs?

Nicole started to step into the cramped space, but Odile put a hand on her shoulder. "Wait," she said, "until you truly need it."

The two sat in the nearest pew, after a quick dusting. Odile hummed a familiar hymn, and Nicole let the notes relax her frayed nerves. If she slipped through Vachon's fingers, what would her next move be?

"This church is a curious circumstance, a conundrum," Nicole said. "Why do you stay?"

"Too old to leave. My time is almost spent," Odile said flatly, no signs of remorse or melancholy.

"You must feel compelled to attend to the occasional need if it arises?" Nicole probed. She sought some measure of reassurance that the spiritual state of the village was not a complete loss.

Odile squeezed Nicole's hand. "Of course I do."

"And what do the villagers think of you?"

"I can't say."

"Oh, don't be modest. They probably hold you most dear if you've stayed through the worst of times."

"I can't say because it would get me in trouble."

Nicole looked more closely at the woman's face, wrinkled by experience. A tiny smile crossed the nun's lips, and the truth became quite clear.

"They think of you as the priest."

Odile's smile neither grew nor faded.

"Yes," Nicole said and matched the woman's smile. "I suppose that's not a fact I would share with just anyone either."

The silence of the shared secret shattered in gunshot.

Nicole ducked and got down on hands and knees. Odile pointed toward the confessional. "Go. Get in. I'll deal with him."

Nicole hesitated, but the nun turned the opposite way and scooted on her knees to the door.

"No shooting allowed!" She yelled toward the entrance.

The confessional and its secret compartment suddenly shrunk. As bad luck would have it, Nicole's belly was an inch too wide for the opening. Saying a prayer for mercy, she did the only thing possible to give herself some extra room and space for the baby. She reluctantly relieved her bladder. The secret door clicked shut.

Her heartbeat filled her ears. The weight of the world laid on this feeble plan, a secret hideout, a skinny door, and a nun probably older than the wood of the confessional. She struggled to listen over the doom pressing down on her.

A boom and crack echoed inside the sanctuary.

"Here now," Odile said, farther away than Nicole remembered the front door being. "No need to burst into the house of God."

"You there," Vachon's voice seemed clearer than a church bell. And excessively agitated. "Get off the floor and show yourself."

Nicole figured Odile had ducked for cover at a second gunshot. Had Vachon fired inside? No way of knowing. She regretted placing the old woman in harm's way. The woman's sacrifice deserved more than Nicole had to offer.

"We don't open the church until far later in the morning, Monsieur. You've ruined the front door for everyone."

What sounded like a short scuffle ensued—the sudden shifts of leather soles and wooden heels across the smooth stone floor, followed by a gasp, and a grunt. *Lord, keep her safe.*

Then there came a *whack whack whack.*

"Good Lord, woman," Vachon said. "Stop trying your altar boy ways with me and sit still. I believe you're harboring a fugitive."

"Even if that were so, your rude behaviour will not be tolerated, neither by me or by my Lord God."

Nicole's breath in the tight box made the space hot. The heat and her dampness soured her hope.

Vachon's heels clicked in one direction and then another. "Where's the priest?" He was on the verge of shouting.

Odile fired back: "Gone."

"Old women are good for two things," Vachon said, stomping off in a new direction, "birthing babies and washing diapers."

"Hmm." Odile probably had done both.

The sound of the man's boot heels diminished until Nicole could not hear them. Odile didn't move, so neither did she. She wanted to whisper something to her rescuer to make sure she was all right, but shifting even a pinkie wasn't going to keep her place a secret.

The clip of the heels returned. Their next direction was toward the confessional.

Nicole took one long breath and froze.

The door to the priest's booth, next to hers, opened with a swift whoosh. Vachon slapped it shut. The next door was hers.

The air pressure in her hideout released a little as the main door flew open. But he didn't close it right away. He was so close, she almost felt his breathing, where each inhale was followed by a frustrated, rushed exhale.

"You need to clean in here, old woman," Vachon said, and finally slammed the door. "Seems your flock has decided to use it as a chamber pot."

"Hmm." Odile must have been a good card player, too.

Nicole let out her breath as the heels headed farther into the church and back to the vicinity where the skirmish started. Vachon demanded Odile show him the priest's study, and they were gone far longer than Nicole feared was safe. But she stuck to her spot and waited them out.

After what seemed like an everlasting moment, the two shuffled back. The sound of his footsteps, slower and less demanding, meant the hunt had lost steam. Nicole made a tiny cross on her forehead with one finger and prayed the ordeal was done.

"Remember what I said, old woman," Vachon said, almost too faintly for Nicole to hear. "The decision you make can have stinging consequences."

More heels, then nothing. The church grew quiet. The folds of Nicole's body streamed with sweat, and her neck and knees ached. Stay still, she urged herself, just a little bit longer.

Odile must have taken off her shoes, because when the door to Nicole's confessional snapped open, she almost cracked her head on the ceiling out of fright. Odile quietly informed her, "He's gone."

# 6

# Freedom Less Joy

Athos whisked Pierre and Grignan from the mayhem at Notre Dame with Camille bringing up the rear. Pierre leaned on Athos and eventually had to be carried. Athos shifted Pierre's weight, slight from near starvation, onto his back and made much better time. The men bobbed through the crowds toward the safest place in Paris, d'Artagnan's empty apartment.

Grignan had suggested it. He'd stayed there while he was in hiding, with d'Artagnan's blessing. The unluckiest of the men, d'Artagnan had spent months away at the front, so the four decided to drink to his health and safety as well as their good luck. A few demijohns of wine were procured in their rush toward safety.

"d'Artagnan would have wanted us here," Camille said, lifting his cup to Pierre and Grignan.

Second pours were made before anyone else spoke.

Pierre was laid on d'Artagnan's modest bed, a cot in a corner with a canvas bottom and a sturdy headboard, a much nicer piece than at Athos's attic. Grignan ministered to his wounds. He had brought along a few personal items, one being a kit of small medicinal herbs and rubs. A curtain was ripped into strips and a balm, made of lard and camphor, was spread on Pierre's hand and the raw scar from the brand. Pierre hardly winced. That meant to Athos his young friend was either too delirious to feel anything, or his tolerance for pain had thickened into an impenetrable dike.

Upon seeing the brand, Athos curled his hands into fists.

"If there's any way you can rid him of the brand, then do it."

Grignan at first took it as a joke until Athos repeated it again, more determined than before.

"Are you suggesting I cut it off?" Grignan stood up from his patient. "Because that's the only way you can get rid of it. I'm not a surgeon, I'll remind you."

"Remove it, before it heals."

"He's hardly in any condition for that," Grignan said. Camille came to stand by the priest.

"He'll never live a free life with that curse on his body," Athos said.

Camille passed in front of Grignan. "Take a good look at him, Athos. He's going to need his strength to make it through the next few days. Cutting off that mark isn't going to help."

"Anything he does from now on will require that he hide it or hope no one ever finds it. It will haunt him. It's a mercy to do it now before it heals. Now. Or doom him forever."

Grignan threw up his hands, and Camille shook his head.

"Give him the rest of the wine," Athos said and handed the last drink from the bottle to Grignan. Not in any hurry, the priest took the wine and urged the young man to sip.

Pierre's eye opened only halfway, and the wine dribbled out of his pale lips.

"And who do you suggest do the honours?" Grignan asked, with a daring tone.

"Me." Athos stepped to the bedside and rummaged through Grignan's kit. A pair of sharp scissors was buried in the bottom.

"For God's sake," Grignan said and held Athos at the wrist. "You can't be serious. Hasn't he been through enough already?"

Athos knelt at the cot and uncovered the temporary bandage from the mark. He wished he'd never known how dire its consequences could be. It could turn a person into a devil, ruin a life and everyone around it. He took the wine and doused the blades of the scissors, then did something he never did.

He sent up a silent prayer.

Pierre wasn't so far gone that he didn't feel Athos begin to cut. His eyes popped open and he sprung up at Athos and clutched both of his arms. The burn on his hand didn't stop him.

Athos braced and kept the scissors positioned on the patch of skin. "Don't! You'll only make it worse."

"You're the devil himself!" Pierre scratched him using the jagged edges of his dirty fingernails.

"Hold him." But the other men seemed frozen by the unfolding tug-of-war. "I said hold him!"

Grignan pressed down on Pierre's shoulders, and Camille pinned his arms to the sides of the cot. Repeating a phrase in Latin, the priest closed his eyes tightly and turned his cheek. Camille watched Athos complete the brutal defacing until blood covered the cot underneath the wound. As soon as the last recognizable sign of the mark was peeled from the skin, Athos ripped his own shirt sleeve off and pressed. Pierre stopped struggling and passed out.

Grignan flopped on the floor the moment the assault ended.

"It's only a surface wound. It'll heal fast," Athos said and tossed the scissors off to one side.

"It's worth remarking," Grignan said, slightly out of breath, "that he never screamed. I take that as a bad omen."

Athos promptly left and wandered off to find another bottle.

∞∞∞

The welt over Odile's left eye began to darken shortly after she helped Nicole from her hiding place.

"Such an intemperate man," Odile said resting on a pew. Her eye grew puffy and squeezed her lids together. "He wanted blood."

"He's hunting my nephew. I'm just a means to an end," Nicole said and joined her on the dusted seat. She inspected Odile's head for other injuries and combed her fingers through the nun's gray hair, away from her ruined face. "I'm so sorry. Please forgive me."

Odile patted Nicole's hand. Laid side by side, their hands were generations apart, and yet Nicole felt a strong connection. "Are there water and rags here?"

Odile rose, and together they left the church for her room. The light helped Nicole see the layout of the church grounds. They'd entered a garden. The entire back of the church was planted from inch to inch. The neat, weeded rows contained vegetable and flower starts. A few sunflowers swayed above their heads.

Last summer, about this time, she had first met the Musketeer. Athos had arrived at her château nearly a broken man. Her curiosity and attraction drew her closer to him as the weeks of the summer unfolded. He hadn't wanted to be in her company at first, tied to an untenable mission for her husband, but the longer he stayed, the greater his desire to be with her. They'd fallen in love.

"Far away, I see." Odile was standing at the open door of her hovel.

Nicole hadn't taken her eyes off the sunflowers. "Yes, missing someone."

Inside, Odile busied herself as if the morning were like any other. Nicole found a suitable rag to dab on Odile's eye, now completely sealed shut. But the old woman wasn't in a mood to stand still. She took the rag from Nicole and sopped up water from a basin and went to scrubbing any unmovable surface.

Nicole became more self-conscious about her soiled clothes. Not that she had an alternative. Fugitives leave in a hurry. Anyway, the place didn't have a curtain or dressing screen, so Nicole just stood by the open door and fanned the back of her skirt.

Odile pulled her back inside, stuck her head out, looked this way and that, then closed and locked the door. "Can't be too careful."

Before Nicole could muster a sigh, Odile handed her a long frock and motioned for her to change. She turned her back and kept scrubbing.

"We'll wash them tomorrow. No rush to leave."

Nicole puzzled at what she meant, whether the nun wanted the extra time and company or whether there was futility in the idea that she could get away. Come to think of it, leaving did pose several problems. Without money, a horse, any sort of bargaining chip except her status as the Comtesse, she might find it hard to get where she wanted to go. And where that was, was Paris.

"Sit," Odile asked of her after Nicole fitted herself into the fresh attire.

Nicole suspected she'd need to tell a better version of events. The woman deserved that, and more. She didn't even bother to wait for the first question.

On the stool, commanding her best posture, she spoke: "The Comte de Rochefort, my husband, is dead because of circumstances involving me and my nephew."

Odile interrupted, "Dead? The Comte? This is news." She took a seat on her bed and scratched the top of one bony knee. "You don't act the part of a murderess."

Nicole leaned forward. "I take responsibility for my part, but it was my nephew who killed him."

"Killed. Hmm."

"My husband was a gambler. His wagers were notorious. His last wager involved the man who ..." She glanced down at her belly and raised her head high. "... a good man, an honourable man, a Musketeer who saved my life."

The nun blinked. Nicole blinked back.

"The Comte involved the Musketeer in a bet at my expense. My husband was really using him for financial gain. My nephew became entangled because he hated the Comte's authority and grew spiteful. I had raised the boy under the pretense that he was a servant when his mother died. My sister had run away with a peasant. Pierre never knew her. He only knew his place in our household as an inferior."

Nicole left the worst details out. The ones few would understand, such as her sister's suicide, she hid in her own conscience.

"Sounds messy," Odile replied. "Not sure it matters to me."

"The man whom you encountered tonight is Vachon. He worked for my husband. His brother Henri tried to hurt me, and my nephew killed him in my defense."

"Killed two? Your husband and another? He's not good with God."

Nicole shook her head. "He's young. Ideas of grandeur are stuck in his head. He wants to be a Musketeer."

"Is he?"

Nicole shook her head.

"Where is he?"

"The Bastille."

Odile didn't say anything. She pinched her bottom lip between her thumb and forefinger, thinking. Her good eye squinted a little, and her contemplation made her appear like she might be nodding off.

"My friend, the Musketeer, is in Paris trying to free him. We've been working to secure his freedom for months by correspondence, but his case is difficult. He killed my husband at a public event in Le Louvre. Both the King and Queen were in attendance."

Odile's face opened up. Even her bruised eye wanted to open. "My, my."

"It's so unbelievable." Nicole dropped her face into her hands and imagined the life-altering night at Le Louvre. That night, her emotions rode from despair to hope to horror in the span of an hour. "I'm still trying to make sense of it."

"This Musketeer," Odile asked, "is he on good terms within his ranks?"

She lifted her head. "The best. Far better than I am in mine."

"I can imagine."

"He left many weeks ago from my care in Rochefort, and I was to await the outcome. Vachon kidnapped me as leverage."

"Nothing for you to do now. Home is where you should be." Odile moved her feet to rise off the bed, but Nicole stopped her.

"You've been so kind. I can't begin to know how to repay you. There is much wealth at my disposal."

"Give it to the poor." Odile got on her feet.

Nicole took the nun's hands in hers. "I need to leave here, and Rochefort is not where I want to be."

"Not sure I agree."

"If I could get to Paris, I'll feel better. I could find Athos, assist in my nephew's release."

"Does anyone want you there?"

No, Nicole thought to herself, not a soul, not even Athos. Prior to Vachon, even she had not wanted to be in Paris. She was a disgrace. But need wanted her loved ones nearer.

"Paris is far away. Rochefort is only a day or two." Odile passed a hand over Nicole's middle. "Need more convincing than this?"

Nicole turned from the nun, ashamed to admit the baby was not a worry. Above the mess, the baby seemed a solid point of calm. Quiet. Growing. The strength of possibility.

The conversation ended. Odile put up her cleaning supplies and prepared a little food. She left the room and returned with a handful of lettuces and stubby carrots. The two sat next to each other and found peace in the sustenance.

# The Trials of an Orphan

Athos stewed for twenty-four hours about whether to leave Pierre under the care of Grignan and search for Nicole himself. The teams of Musketeers who had been dispatched across the countryside to find her were still days away from reporting any news. It agitated him into a fit of drinking.

The wine was a poor companion. It dulled his ability to think level-headedly about anything—Nicole, his rescue plan, Pierre's future. Then there was the vengeful duo of Geneviève and Vachon, the Devil's soldiers. Because nothing else seemed to make any sense, he concocted an elaborate story in his head about how the two evildoers had met. It hinged on lust.

Pierre slept for the entire time that Athos binged. Camille joined him for a few rounds then doubled up with Grignan to find a physician who might agree to see Pierre without turning him back over to the authorities.

Athos tossed a finished bottled into a pile in the corner of d'Artagnan's apartment, and the clinking sound aroused Pierre. His eyes blinked at the daylight from the small windows over the bed. Athos pulled the curtains and dragged a seat over to the bedside.

"Remember me?" Athos asked.

Pierre's lids moved slowly up and down, and his grogginess threatened to take him down again. Athos wanted him to stay awake, so he squeezed his bandaged hand.

"Hey," Pierre finally said in his defense. "Stop."

"Wake up. We must talk," Athos said.

"No. Sleep." Pierre might have well been a breeze, as soft as he sounded.

"I need to tell you things you may not know."

Pierre's eyes found Athos's. An understanding passed between them, but Pierre grumbled in distaste. "Sleep."

"You can get all the sleep you want after we speak. I want to talk to you before the others return."

"You cut me."

"Yes, for very good reason."

"You're a bastard."

Athos laughed to himself. The Pierre he knew and loved still simmered beneath the surface.

"It was either that or live as a branded man the rest of your life, or until you figured out a way to rid yourself of the brand without a worse scar." Athos lifted Pierre's shirt. Grignan had relented earlier, out of sheer mercy, to sew the cut, even though Athos was more experienced with wounds. The priest's conscience had gotten the better of him.

Pierre also bore the mark of another assault that Athos unfortunately had caused the first day they had met.

"Admiring your handiwork?" Pierre rolled away from Athos's reach.

"If we keep this up, you'll be as scarred as I am."

"Not likely."

"I'll never wish that for you," Athos said. "Neither will Nicole. She sends her immense love. She's been on a faithful prayer vigil and overcome with worry."

"Worry and inaction."

Athos frowned. It was just like Pierre to blame them. "We've been writing anyone who might have the slightest sway in your case for months. The fact remains that you killed an innocent man, an aristocrat, in the most public way possible, and in the presence of your King and Queen. Not much could be done. That doesn't lessen the injustices reaped upon you. Our country will regret that unjust place in history for centuries to come."

"Then pity the French fools," Pierre said sardonically.

Athos rubbed his hands down his face. "You're alive and free. God must be merciful."

Pierre turned his face to the wall. "The Comte was not innocent."

"You and I agree on that point." Athos nodded. "Listen, Pierre, there are more things you must know about yourself, and Nicole is adamant that you know them."

"Save it. I've heard the story already."

"I know, but she has sent with me property that really belongs to you."

"So."

"There are letters here. Letters from your mother. From Sibonne. She wrote to you knowing she wouldn't live to see you become a man."

Pierre jerked his head toward the Musketeer. His grogginess had vanished. "Did you read them?"

"No, and neither has Nicole," Athos said. "They've been sealed for eighteen years."

Pierre's eyes darted around the room. Athos thought he might leap from the bed in search of them. From under the mattress, Athos produced the thin stack. Fewer than a dozen letters were bound by a black ribbon.

Pierre snatched them away. Athos saw a ghost dance in Pierre's eyes.

A moment of hesitation gripped the young man. Having lived many more years and learned life's lessons, Athos felt a tinge of pity. Knowledge was frequently wrapped in a coarse lining. God had designed the world that way, a union of harshness and light.

The young man slowly shrunk back from his enthusiasm. Athos placed a hand on his shoulder.

"Remember, your father is alive, Pierre. He knows about you. He may be able to fill in what's missing."

Pierre's sour mood returned. "He doesn't care."

"Because he's hurt. He made mistakes, and he doesn't know you yet. Go find him. He told me to tell you that. He needs to know that you are his son, from top to bottom."

"It won't matter," Pierre said, his hands loosening their grip on the stash of letters. "I'm still a bastard. A criminal."

"You have us. And always will." Athos said it regardless of whether it would take root.

"What of you?" Pierre stabbed the question. "I've been starved and abused for months, and you were where?"

A smattering of guilt washed over Athos. He granted Pierre his moment.

"All I get at the end of that Hell is this?!" Pierre raised the letters and crumpled them in half. "Letters from a mother whose death places the curse of melancholia upon me? There's nothing you can say that will take away that shame or the pain of the Bastille …"

Pierre winced and abruptly lost headwind. The pain in his hand and side slowed down his ranting. But Athos had to give Pierre one more piece of bad news about Nicole, who needed their support far more urgently than they needed to lick their wounds.

"Rest," he said instead. "I'm needed elsewhere. I know you'll heal in Grignan's care. But heed me, if you do nothing else, be careful and watch your back. There are people here in Paris seeking vengeance. My best advice to you is leave the city as soon as you're able. Find the gypsy they call Reginald roaming in the southern provinces. He's probably expecting you."

And with that, Athos gathered a few provisions and left the young man to his own devices.

∞∞∞∞

Pierre ground the words of the Musketeer into powder. They were as good as dust between cracks of cobblestone.

He credited Grignan for his freedom. Athos had arrived too late. The Musketeer just happened to be at the right place at the right time at Notre Dame. Pierre clenched the letters for a second or two before the pain in his hand prevented more.

*Letters!* She had written him letters. Messages from the grave. What could they possibly say to change his circumstances? What coherent thoughts could a mad woman articulate?

There were eight, ink faint and paper yellowing. She'd handwritten his name, and underneath she'd lettered the date. One each month the year after his birth. Her cursive was plain except for the first letters of his name. She'd added flourishes to the P and the T. Maybe it spoke to how his life was evolving. An elaborate beginning that trailed off into plain obscurity.

He'd entered the realm of the discarded. The downtrodden. The muck of society.

The months in the Bastille demonstrated his true worth. No one cared whether he lived or died. In a peculiar way now, he felt more alone than he had in the dungeon. Why? No answer sounded right. Life tatters, he thought, and mending becomes impossible. You always have a void. You re-weave new fabric or perish.

He flipped the first letter around a few times and contemplated burning it. Like Nicole, Sibonne hadn't cared enough either. His mother let her sister raise him. He didn't even know Nicole was her sister until she finally broke down and told him, right before he killed the Comte. Maybe that's why he ended up murdering him. His life story tainted his view of everything. The lies about his past had gone on too long, and the truth didn't set him free. It launched him into freefall.

The waxy adhesive on the letter barely stuck when he opened the first.

His mother's voice pierced him in the first line.

*Pierre, You are my son. I have let you go. There is an ache in me that will not cease. What I did may seem unfathomable. It is and was. I did it to keep you safe—hidden from the harm of men far too powerful for my station. You see, I am a fallen woman. I chose to follow my heart, and suffering is my plight. I suffer knowing you sleep away from my bosom. I suffer knowing you'll never gaze at me and smile. I survive on the knowledge that your father has you. He will do as we have agreed and see that your life thrives. These are my wishes for you: grow strong, believe in yourself, help others, and love as fiercely as I love you. Your mother, Sibonne Tremon*

Pierre cursed himself. Opening the letter had been a mistake. She wanted to be the sympathetic character, the tragic female in the play. Her one-sided account ensured she enshrined herself in a role that he could never recast. The role was her own making.

He tossed the other letters to the floor, curled into a ball, and pushed the words out of his mind.

∞∞∞

Athos rounded the street to find Camille running in his direction. He ran full speed until he reached the Musketeer, who caught him. Bending over, panting to catch his breath, Camille wheezed out a few words. "Gone … Grignan … they found him."

Athos pulled up his friend and squarely understood the reality of their loss.

"When?"

"Not sure," Camille said, puffing. "I ran from the gates of the Bastille to get here."

"You think that's where they found him, and who exactly?"

"Don't know." Camille leaned over, squeezing his side. "He was late for our rendezvous. The later it got, the clearer it became that he wasn't coming."

Athos pounded a fist into a hand. "He's not worth anything to them!"

"Only information. Seems strange. Wrong time, wrong place." Camille leaned against the building and wiped sweat from his brow.

"Nothing's going our way."

"We have Pierre."

"Only in body. I hate to leave you with him."

"He's young. And injured. He'll snap out of it."

"I intend to find Nicole."

Camille nodded, but not as an endorsement. "I gathered that much."

Athos looked up at the apartment window. "He's full of bitterness. His attitude is as foul as pig waste. And he doesn't know that a scorned lover and a vengeful brother are after him. Maybe you'll not endure the brunt of it. Once he's a little better, you should probably move him to my quarters on the Rue Férou to be safe."

Camille gave Athos a few coins from his pocket. "Here."

Athos tossed him a thankful smile. "I'll make a few inquiries of Grignan first. Then, I must find her."

"Yes, you must," Camille said. At the doorway, he shouted back. "That money is not for wine, in case you needed reminding."

# 8

# Cooking Up A Plan

Nicole spent the day in hiding. Neither she nor Odile could decide if Vachon believed the nun's story. Nicole wasn't interested in underestimating him or taking chances. Odile kept the door open to her room and tended the garden while Nicole watched from the shadows inside.

The fresh vegetables quenched Nicole's hunger. Odile prepared her sliced tomatoes and basil drizzled with oil. There were steamed greens and small potatoes for the evening meal that the nun grilled over an open fire pit. The rudimentary nature of the old woman's existence appealed to Nicole's quiet sensibilities. She often had visions of herself as an old lady wandering through the woods on her land, looking for wild mushrooms and medicinal herbs.

"Does the priest ever come around?" Nicole wondered out loud, cognizant of her volume.

"Depends," the nun said, sweeping the threshold of her hardened dirt floor after dinner. "Wine's what he wants, and we don't have any."

"Why don't you stay inside the church?"

"Then no one would know where I am."

It seemed an odd answer. They hadn't seen or heard anyone the entire day.

"I know what you're thinking," she said, acknowledging Nicole's skepticism. "No one comes around, so what's keeping her from the run of the place? My own conscience, that's what."

Nicole watched the woman sweep. Her broom was sure. Her ideas, surer.

"If you have an opinion about how I might be able to leave here," Nicole said, "I'm open to hearing it."

"Wait. You need to wait longer."

"An eternity wouldn't be long enough. Until Vachon has tracked down Pierre, I'll stay a target."

Odile took a few more swipes at the floor, then stuck the broom in a corner. She beat her skirt free of cling-on dust particles and rummaged around until she found her book of devotionals.

"What did you think?" Odile held up the cover to Nicole.

She wasn't in the mood for religious discourse or a change in subject, but she spoke her mind.

"I'm not sure it conveys anything different than what I've read in traditional texts. Many of the passages sounded identical to teachings I've heard and read my entire life."

A smile broader than any she'd seen for weeks crossed the nun's face.

"Ha! And you'd be right." She clapped the book twice in the air, and the slaps caused Nicole to blink hard. "It's a decoy."

"Pardon me?"

"A decoy, milady! The Ursaline's version of a red herring."

Nicole caught herself in a hesitant giggle. "I'm not sure I follow."

Odile dragged the stool over to the bed and prepared herself for a long story.

"It happened that my order came under scrutiny. From the Cardinal himself."

"Richelieu."

"The grand man in red. He may put on a good front, spouting lofty talk of art and progress, but he's got the political hide of a rhinoceros." Odile chuckled, then reeled her enthusiasm back in. "He didn't care for our little band, right under his hat, at the abbey of Saint Germain-de-Prés."

"Saint Germain? You lived at Saint Germain?"

"Of course I did. You know it?"

"More intimately than most," Nicole said.

"Then you may also know," she said before a darting glance of paranoia toward the door, "that secretly many of the monks and nuns, former nuns, held beliefs that broadened the teachings of the church. We wanted more women to be teachers, in particular, teachers of religion. Rebels, we were."

"When did you live there?"

"Oh, many, many years ago. Cast out with the lot of them."

"Richelieu sent you away?"

"More or less. Our ideas got under his tough skin."

"But your devotional ..."

"Was one of our last attempts to persuade him, and several other skeptics, that we weren't a threat. It's a word-for-word reprint of a devotional from the time of Henry the Fifth." Again, a short chuckle.

"Doesn't presenting someone else's work as your own qualify as a sin? You were lying to the Cardinal or everyone who read it, for that matter."

"Hmm. No. We didn't reject those ideas, we believed they needed to be expanded and sent out by us." Odile poked her chest and hopped the stool a few inches closer to the bed.

"When he 'cast you out,' what happened to you?"

"Not worth retelling," she said, looking away from Nicole's eyes, "but we vowed in those last days not to stop talking. I walked all the way here from Paris. Weeks it took. Every small town I stayed in, every family who opened its arms, I taught the women and young girls the same instruction."

"You taught them to find their voice."

Odile excitedly patted Nicole's knee. "I was right about you. You understand."

"I've taught several of my servants to read."

"You're a miracle, my dear!"

"Oh, I wouldn't go that far."

"Hmm. I saw it in you the minute we met."

"A displaced woman with child but without a coach, a miracle?"

"Self-assurance. Resilience. A woman with an idea or two in her head. We need more like you."

"Yet here I am. Cornered into a confinement that has no clear exit. I haven't a single notion about what to do next."

"Ah, rest." The nun got off the stool and placed the devotional on a shelf near the door. "There's more to being an exiled Ursaline than publishing usurped doctrine. One of the serendipitous outcomes of being castoff is the knowledge of how to sneak out of a church without getting caught."

∞∞∞

Athos darted through the city to the headquarters of Cardinal Richelieu's guard, not the most welcome place for a Musketeer. But he had no recent run-ins with the Cardinal's men, so his inquiries about Grignan needed to start there. The guards would be in charge of the unwilling recruits being carted off to Prague.

A few guardsmen took notice of Athos as soon as he stepped onto the grounds of the compound and took no time considering whether to approach him. Much like the Musketeer's headquarters in another quarter of Paris, the place stewed in ego and bravado.

"You there," a large man in uniform said on his way across the practice yard, first in a pack of three. It was Jussac, an old rival of Athos, but who among them wasn't? "Musketeers should keep to the gallows, or should I say, on the gallows."

Their snide laughs drew attention from a few others, but Athos expected that much.

"I'm not here to parry, just find a prisoner."

"As you can see, we're all men here, not miscreants," Jussac fired back. "You Musketeers keep horrible company."

"I'd say," another yelled from a second group of men. Another familiar, Biscarat. "That's the Musketeer who seduced the Comtesse de Rochefort."

The three nearest him took a closer look at his face. "The one they call Athos?" a third asked.

A few more men started gathering around his back. The wind had changed, and Athos's compass spun. Where it would stop wasn't entirely clear.

"So, are you … ?" Jussac asked.

"I am Athos." He anchored his feet to the ground. "Don't you remember me?"

"Maybe I do," he said, turning his head to view more of the Musketeer's profile, "and maybe I don't."

"He looks smitten. Soft!" a guard yelled from behind Jussac.

"And all those stories about you—seducing the Comtesse, teaching that young peasant to fence, the one who killed her husband—those are true?"

Whether or not they believed his answer didn't matter. The truth always favoured the storyteller's version of events.

"If I reply truthfully, might I ask a favour?"

By now, the majority of the men in the vicinity had gathered around the brewing scene. He commanded the spotlight. He rarely asked for it; it followed him without permission.

Several of the men discussed Athos's proposal. They shot him sharp looks and knowing nods. Their verdict might be perilous or a seal of brotherhood. The Royalists and the Cardinalists usually had little to gain from cooperation.

"Show us the scar first," Biscarat said, "the one that nearly killed you."

Alas, that part of the story had grown in proportion since his absence from Paris life, too. The only reason Athos hadn't killed the Comte himself was because he had been critically wounded on the shoulder. The wound of a gypsy's arrow. It almost caused his fighting arm to go lame. During an ambush, the injury nearly ended his life.

He bared one shoulder, where the arrow had gone out. Most of the men shook their heads, seeing the scar tissue confirmed the outlandish tale.

"Are you still as good with a sword?" Jussac asked.

"Earlier in the day."

Another man in the back shouted: "So you won't be entering Le Prix du Fer any time soon."

His silence caused the entire innyard to rumble in laughter.

"See here, the man hasn't been living in Paris for what … more than a year? How would he know of Le Prix?" Jussac said, touting his insider's knowledge.

"What I've heard hasn't stirred my interest," Athos said.

"Nor should it," Jussac provoked. "It's a secret match to the death for only the finest French swordsmen and not for those soft in the middle."

"Regardless of my ability or interest, I believe you owe me a favour." He approached the request tentatively, testing the water. "I'm in search of a priest who may have mistakenly been thrown in with the prisoners headed to the conflict."

"A priest? Does this have anything to do with the Comtesse, the woman who's made you soft?"

Although irritated, Athos chose not to lie. When appealing to a Frenchman, love was always an excellent sympathy card.

"In truth, it does," he said.

"This story gets better and better," Jussac said and snorted approval. Several of the men grunted their agreement.

"Father Grignan helped her when she was most in need. We owe him much, and he's missing."

"And then you helped *her* when she was most in need," Biscarat chided. After the laughs faded, several men asked, in one way or another: *What's the priest's name?*

"Grignan. Simon Grignan."

Nothing but silence. A few shook their heads.

"He went missing this afternoon. He may be considered a fugitive, but I can't divulge why. There may be others who want his head."

"His head?" Biscarat shook his. "He must be in some foul pot, and you can't seem to stay out of them either." He paused thinking over the news. "What if we make you a deal?"

Athos liked a good gamble. In this company, chance favoured the man most determined to win.

"We'll look for your priest on the condition that you stay out of Le Prix," Biscarat said, turning to the others who nodded in approval. "The glory and prize money are only ours to seek."

Athos's status as the longest living Musketeer effectively made him the favourite in any duel, especially one as spectacularly notorious as Le Prix seemed to be. He mostly wanted to avoid glory fighting, so the offer sounded like the perfect arrangement.

And in many ways, he felt his days as a Musketeer could be winding to a close. His life with Nicole was far too precious to sacrifice for a cause less than the King's life.

"Agreed," he said.

Back slaps and cheers filled the compound.

"And if you don't stay out of it," Jussac warned, "we'll kill you without regard for the rules."

∞∞∞

The search for Grignan was on, in earnest. The Cardinal's guards were as good as their word. He blithely took their threat as an act of chest-pounding. Equally, he took it as a compliment, for fear of his superiority in a duel. Rather than feel concerned, his spirits were lifted. His next move, however, held far less promise.

To find Nicole, he needed answers. The one person who had them also expected him. The deadline to comply with Geneviève's demands to hand over Pierre had arrived.

She entered her parlour like she had before, in full plumage.

"You please me more than I can say," she said and sat across the loveseat. Her dress, a deep crimson trimmed in black, set off her striking dark hair. "You don't care much for women like me, do you?"

"I prefer less showy."

"Humility?"

"No," he said and sat at the desk. "Authenticity."

She burst into a short clip of throaty laughter, but it was a defense for his well-placed aim.

"So," she said, twirling the end of a ribbon that cinched her bosom into two perfect plums, "have you saved your precious Nicole?"

"I will."

"Oh, let me guess, you have everyone at your disposal searching for her from field to farm. Don't go to all that trouble, Monsieur. In fact, why not have a little fun in her absence?"

She came off the loveseat and strode to the desk where she plucked the quill out of its stand and traced the feather along the line of her cleavage up to her painted lips. The aroma off her skin was that of a row of prized white roses near her front door.

Not a thing about her attracted him. In fact, there were dangerous shades of Milady de Winter in Geneviève. She wanted his genuine attention perhaps more than she realized.

He spoke honestly. "You're lonely."

Her face flattened, defying gravity. "I enjoy the attention of many."

"But you're not satisfied. You're not in love."

"The Comte loved—"

"The Comte loved his wife," he said. "It's why he didn't leave her. I dare say it ate away your heart."

Again, his aim was impeccable. Her confident glow wilted. She rammed the quill back inside the stand. "Monsieur, your tongue is dangerously close to being cut out."

"Tell me," he said, "when did you realize the Comte wasn't going to leave her?"

She opened her mouth to speak but snapped it shut. Her jaw clinched.

He jumped on the extended pause. "You despise women like Nicole, a woman truly unlike yourself. Untainted by Court intrigues."

"This isn't winning you any points, Monsieur," she said, or rather, seethed.

"But if you could get back at her, you would," Athos said and took a quick glance around the parlour. "Did the Comte love you beyond measure?"

No answer.

"You say you want Pierre," he said, straight toward her, "but everything tells me your greatest desire is to exact revenge on Nicole."

Leaning over the desk, he waited for her to crack.

She smiled and suddenly jabbed the quill into his hand. A jolt of pain ran up his arm before he could pull it out. He threw it at her retreating back and compressed the wound. "I've known women like you," he growled, "but they were far more subtle in their hatred."

Her full-blown pride made a reprise. She waltzed around the room with perfect timing. She smiled, but agitation simmered beneath her calm. "Perhaps I do want her to suffer more than anyone."

Athos pressed the small puncture harder.

"Handing Pierre over is the only way you'll ever see her again."

"If you can find him. He's free," Athos said, a blatant lie to confound her, "and in control of his own destiny."

"What?" Geneviève switched course right for him. The swishing of her skirt roiled like a thunder cloud. "How do you know this?"

He stood his ground. "We helped him escape."

"If you want Nicole back, you'll hand him over this very night!"

"He left my company as soon as he could. I can no more control a headstrong teenager than I can you."

"Where is he?!" She grabbed his wounded hand and dug her nails. "If you don't bring him to me, she'll suffer cruelly!"

He yanked it back. "Give me information about Nicole, and I'll tell you what I know of Pierre."

Her black hair resembled the hood of an executioner. Cold ferocity radiated from every hard line of her face. "You're not in a position to bargain," she retorted.

She stomped toward the desk and scrambled for a note and the inkwell. She fumed when she realized the quill was on the floor, ringed with blood. She shrieked out of frustration. Any more road blocks, and Athos presumed she would throw a temper tantrum.

He picked up the quill and steadily handed it over. She grabbed the nib, but he didn't let go. "Tell me where she is," he said, then lied again, "and I'll lead you to the part of the city where Pierre hides. If you capture him, he's all yours."

"I won't bargain when I hold the ace in my hand! If you want Nicole whole, you must do *my* bidding. You've gambled poorly by setting him free." She slammed the desk drawer shut. "If you know where he is, then bring him here. Or you'll both have her blood on your hands."

He worried she was right, that he was taking a huge risk, but he wasn't about to hand Pierre over to anyone. "Then that leaves me no choice but to find her myself," Athos said and headed for the door.

She called to him. "You're making a deadly mistake."

Before exiting, he made a final volley. "I'm confident my ability to rescue her is greater than your cunning. I rarely lose, Madame."

Her upper lip twitched, a sure sign Athos was digging her wounds.

"If Pierre is off the table," she said, more measured than before, "I have one last proposition. You can save Nicole and win me a fortune in the doing."

∞∞∞

Later that night, Athos argued with Camille about what to do. Should he enter the duel to buy time for the search parties and trust that Geneviève would free Nicole in exchange for the prize money? Or should he leave Paris and find her himself?

Both scenarios possibly led to death; either his or hers. In reality, neither could live without the other. Despite his wish to put his blade aside for good, he favoured the duel.

"You're an idiot to think that's the best choice," Camille said in a small tavern they'd been basting in over the course of the argument.

"It's the least risky of the two," Athos said, more clear-headed from wine than the average drunk. "At least I have more control over the outcome, and it delays any harm that might be done to Nicole until the end of the tournament."

"You're placing a lot of faith in a woman who's abducted the mother of your child. If we leave Paris now, we have a good three days before the first round and that might be just enough time to recover her. Searching for her yourself is the only guarantee she won't be touched."

Athos swiveled in his seat to face Camille and spoke in the gravest tone. "If she dies because I make the wrong choice, I die, too. Not a man on this continent would deny that truth."

The exchanged ended there. Despite his insatiable need to find her, he rewarded a half-sauced plebian a few coins to deliver his decision to Geneviève: He would enter Le Prix.

# Camouflage and Fate

The nun fed Nicole from her garden for a week. Near the end of the seventh day, Nicole's anxious desire to leave overrode Odile's quiet concern. The old woman had particular skills at changing the subject from planning her escape to anything else, probably a defensive skill she had developed as an Ursaline to sidestep sticky situations and interrogations by superiors.

Nicole surprised Odile by joining her in the garden that late afternoon and following her along the rows, weeding. It hit the mark. The nun got nervous.

"You'll ruin your chances of a clean escape, Madame," Odile said, squinting at the gate and the vines running up the walls around the garden. "Out here in plain sight, not good."

The strength behind Nicole's whisper surprised even her. "I must go. Vachon hasn't been sighted anywhere in days. Now is my chance, whatever that chance may be or help you may grant."

The knees of Odile's skirt were damp from ground-in dirt. The weight of the dark patches misshaped the pleat and gave her the appearance of the lowliest of peasants. Her gray hair and eyebrows stood out in stray wires curling from her face. Nicole needed this resourceful woman's help, but pushing for an outcome conflicted with her gratitude. She could be without any advocate.

"Got everything we need," Odile said and tossed the last handful of weeds onto a pile by the potato patch. "Next, we wait for the boy."

An adolescent boy, all arms and legs, exchanged messages with Odile from time to time through the gate to barter for small bunches of radishes or greens. He was keeping an eye out in the village for the strange man who'd been seen asking around for a wandering woman.

"Wait?" Nicole added no filter to her frustration.

"Inside," Odile said, escorting Nicole in by the hand. "You must be prepared."

The nun told Nicole to change out of her clothes, which had been washed earlier in the week and secretly hung out to dry. Those were rolled into a tight bundle, covered with a cheese cloth, and tied by a scrap of fraying rope. Instead, Nicole was to wear the frock the nun had loaned her, and the slack in the garb was gathered up by knots in the back of the fabric. Odile pulled Nicole's hair into a loose bun. When she stepped back to inspect her work, the verdict was, "Hmm."

"Could you please tell me what we are doing?"

Odile peered out the door of her room and said nothing. Nicole dropped onto the bed and said a little prayer, something to the effect that she hoped the nun wasn't absolutely out of her mind.

The rattling sound of the boy tumbling into the gate sucked the awkwardness out of the air.

"He has it!" Odile disappeared from the doorway, and Nicole debated whether to peek. She heard the creak as the gate opened, and fear ran an instantaneous ache up her body and into the back of her head. She didn't want to be seen, but wouldn't the nun have hidden her if someone, even the boy, was expected?

A repetitive squeak came from the garden. A bump and a roll. A squeak and more rolling. A cart? Without a horse? Nicole got into the darkest corner of the room and held her breath.

Odile's head popped into the door. Her eyes blinked to adjust to the low light until they focused on the occupant in the corner.

"It's time to leave."

Working up her courage, Nicole got to the door, peered around it, and took a sudden breath, or maybe a gasp. An enormous wheelbarrow darkened a dusty patch in the dirt. Not a cart, but almost the size of one.

Odile cracked another of her rare wide smiles. "The biggest in the village. Ours for the afternoon."

The boy was nowhere in sight; the gate was relocked.

"Time," the nun said, taking Nicole by the hands, "we must get you in it."

Nicole gulped and didn't move. Odile walked around and around the implement staring at it as if it were a sculptural masterpiece, the finest artwork in France. "Once we have you tightly packed in the bottom, the rest is camouflage."

The camouflage: a week's worth of weeds and compost from their meals.

A light-headedness passed over Nicole, and before she dropped involuntarily, she lowered herself onto the garden bed.

"Now, now, don't drain the communion canter before the altar boy is finished!" Odile dusted off her hands and assisted Nicole off the ground. "You'll be as snug as a bed bug. A little smelly, but we must sacrifice."

The nun gently guided her to first sit, then recline, then mold her body to the shape of the bottom of the barrel. It curved to her body more snugly than she imagined it would. Her belly was cushioned by the bundle of her clothes.

Before the nun started topping her with the limp pile, Nicole stuck up her head. "How will I breathe?"

"Don't worry, I'll leave a hole." The nun tapped her nose and offered a small comfort. "Remember, I've done this before."

The nun took several minutes to arrange the compost over Nicole. Like weaving a basket or the seat for an essential chair, Odile carefully layered Nicole with a blanket of invisibility. True to her promise, she left a hole in the covering, and the air going into Nicole's lungs took on the smell and consistency of thick tea. The pile didn't smell much worse than wet hay. For a while, Nicole could tolerate the strange camouflage.

Its compactness helped her stay calm. Similar to an extra layer of blankets, the organic cover muffled sound and surrounded her in a protective cocoon. A memory of jumping in piles of leaves with Sibonne ran through her thoughts. When the nun lifted and pushed the wheelbarrow, the warm images were quickly replaced with another memory she had of her sister, the time Sibonne had locked her in a hope chest. The anxiety of that claustrophobic hour erased her positive attitude.

Once out the gate, the nun took up humming as she placed each small foot forward toward freedom. Nicole's only sense of what was happening was the jostling of the wagon, the nun's steps, and the occasional sound from the street. She heard informal conversations from afar, a greeting or two, and a dog, whose nose nearly found her air hole. Only needles of light penetrated the weeds and garden waste. Her head bumped the wood bottom a time or two after a deep dip by the front wheel. Once after a particularly deep drop, she heard the nun whisper, "Parbleu."

Their destination was a mile from the village. A sheep herder's farm. Nicole worried it was too far to push such a heavy load. Together, her weight and the garden pile required a sturdy field worker. Odile stopped for her first break as soon as voices no longer seemed close. She'd been smart to pack a pouch of water. Nicole's throat longed for a sip.

Another stretch went by uneventfully. The sound of racing feet quickly came up to the side of the lumbering contraption. Nicole relaxed when the boy spoke, and she silently blessed him for bringing the fateful wheelbarrow to the nun.

"Let me help," the eager youngster insisted.

"Spills too easy," the nun said, not taking a break in her forward motion to give the boy a chance.

"I'm plenty strong enough, and you shouldn't do so much hard work, Odi." His eager feet danced around both sides of the barrel.

*Odi?* Nicole stopped herself from a short burst of laughter. The nickname sounded ill-suited.

"Jonah, run ahead and tell your father my extra plot of vegetables ripened early, and I'll be there soon."

The boy's feet dashed off and slipped into silence, and the lumbering jerks of the wheelbarrow softened. Odile breathed heavily, and she dropped the back legs of the wheelbarrow to the ground. Another drink. From Nicole's estimation, they still had halfway to go.

Nicole wanted to speak and tell the nun to let the boy help, to pull off to the side so she could get out and walk. But they'd argued about sticking to a plan of no talking, no walking. No matter what happened, Odile argued, they weren't safe until they made it to the second hiding place outside of Avrillé. Sweating, Nicole set aside better judgment and stayed agonizingly quiet. Soon, she'd be passing from one compassionate household to another. Except the second had a horse and wagon and was willing to use it to help a stranger. One important point they hadn't discussed in the preparations was where the sheep farmer would take her. Nicole still wanted to go to Paris, but Odile had ignored the subject.

The nun resumed pushing the wagon and walking forward again. Slower, less bumpy. The path turned quieter, grass most likely, and the wheels swished in passing. Before it seemed time for another water break, motion ground to a halt. For a moment, Nicole guessed the nun was fatigued from the weight. The drumming sound of horse's hooves quickly sunk her hope.

It wasn't one horse but several. Nicole imagined Vachon, rejoined with a band of desperate vagrants, who had returned on the promise of easy money. Odile's good camouflage stood a chance of working, but Nicole never placed faith in chance. She locked her warm hands together and hugged her knees even tighter into her chest. If anyone dug down, the mother with child would be something they'd never forget uncovering.

"God have mercy," Odile said. "Did you say your special friend was a Musketeer?"

Nicole didn't know whether to nod, speak, or poke a finger through the hole to test the winds of fate. The horse's hooves were upon them before she could decide. In a manner, she was under too much duress to assume good fortune.

"Ho there!" a confident man's voice shouted in the direction of the women. Nicole estimated three, perhaps four horsemen in the group from the sound of the hooves. "Are you the nun from the village?"

*Speak the truth,* Nicole sent the silent message through the weeds.

A second man spoke. "We've been sent from Paris to find a person of nobility who is missing. We think she may have come this way."

"Are you all Musketeers?" Odile asked, a high-pitched note of skepticism in her voice.

"We are," the first said. "I'm Longdac, the sergeant in charge. Many from Paris are dispatched on this mission."

"By the King?"

"By our most senior member, Athos."

Nicole gasped and punched her fist through the airhole. Feeling the cool outside air on her arm made her realize how hot she'd grown underneath the pile.

A scuffling of horses and feet and muttered astonishments unfolded in the next minute as Nicole was dug from the heap and planted on solid ground. Her appearance, flush and gamely plucked, initiated a round of chuckles from the three horsemen and, eventually, Odile. Nicole blushed. She rushed through a short version of her story, including the escape from the drunken Vachon.

"This story," said the grinning sergeant, "won't be believed."

After a few minutes of congratulatory quips and Nicole's personal thanks to each of the men, Odile recovered their wits and convinced them to move along rather than stay out in broad daylight. She led the group the last half mile to the sheep herder's farm, where she was expected, per her clandestine agreement with the farmer. Nicole and Odile shared a horse while one of the Musketeer's pushed the barrel, or rather humored them by weaving off and on the trail, regaling them with the story he'd retell in Paris about discovering the wealthiest woman in France beneath a pile of garden rubbish. Nicole was flattered to be the butt of a joke that ended well. She welcomed any gossip about her that detracted from the sordid story of her husband's death. Though the longer she outlived him, the less she believed she would outlive the consequences.

At the farm, the party was greeted enthusiastically and also with a degree of caution. Everyone was rushed inside before the farmer would settle down to hear the tale. Rounds of laughter filled the small cottage, bringing Nicole back to an even-keel. She changed out of the soiled garb and listened to the story a second and third time, each from a different Musketeer. Their good nature and humor filled a void, the separation she had suffered from her own beloved solider. She wanted more information about him but not in front of the whole group. Once the farmer's family started preparations for a meal, Nicole took Longdac aside.

"Please tell me any news you have of Paris," she said.

"You mean, of Athos," the sergeant said, smiling at her coyness.

She nodded.

"He rallied us behind your cause."

Her heart grew a fraction. "Do you know of his plan to free my nephew, Pierre?"

"He took it upon himself to head it up, but with whom and by what means, I have no knowledge."

"Has he had any success?"

"We were dispatched before he had time to start."

"He must have made headway by now," Nicole said, fishing for moral support rather than confirmation. The sergeant shook his head.

"I want you to deliver me to him," she said. "I'm useless in Rochefort."

"She's already warned me that you'd say that," he said and nodded to Odile, who dutifully worked in the kitchen with the others. "I agree with her. There's nothing you can do there to help. One of us will assure you are taken back home and guarded until he can return to you."

She frowned, pulling her disappointment inward. "Were those his wishes, too?"

"His wish was for you, and your child, to be brought to safety."

Nicole hugged her belly. "How did Athos know I'd been abducted?"

"By quite a legendary manipulator in Court, the niece of Henry the Fifth, Geneviève de Montpensier. Do you know of her?"

*Know of her? More or less. My husband's mistress.*

"I've never met her," Nicole said, a statement of fact. "And Vachon, has he been found?"

"Not to my knowledge." He touched her arm. "She and this Vachon sound like a murderous pair. If they're both in Paris, you're not safe there. I hope for your sake they are both brought to justice. But, the longer I do my duties, the more I find that those in power usually operate above most edicts."

Nicole thanked him again and joined the group preparing the meal. But it was just in body, not in mind, that she participated.

The late afternoon victory meal—aged sheep's cheese, fresh figs, dried salted pork, and local wine—satisfied everyone but Nicole. For years, she'd lived in seclusion in Rochefort, in part hiding from society and from her husband. Now she felt driven to the very vortex she despised—the heart of Parisian society. It was easy to avoid Court when no one she loved participated.

She followed Odile out to the barn once the festivities died down; the nun had agreed to throw the food scraps to the farm animals. Odile changed the subject before Nicole got far into her speech. She just wanted the old woman's blessing, if nothing else.

"God bless the animals," Odile kept saying, her back to Nicole.

"Odile, please understand. I must go to Paris."

The nun clucked her tongue at the skittish chickens in the barnyard.

"You're a reasonable person," Nicole tried again. "Listen to reason."

"Reason? Or heartache? Don't let it make decisions for you."

Nicole turned Odile around by the shoulders.

"Remember when you told me I had an idea or two in my own head?"

The old woman's mouth puckered into a sour puss.

"Why must we always do as we are told?" Nicole argued. "The meek, the lesser sex, the servant of man. I'm capable of making decisions about my future, and this turn of events requires I do as my heart instructs."

"So you agree with me! You are making this choice because of your heart not your head. A mistake. Women need to use their brains."

"How will I do any good sitting on the side, waiting for an outcome? I have money and that should be my sword and shield."

"You've been abducted once. Your money did you no good. You risk too much." She turned back to the gathering chickens.

"Odile," Nicole said calmly though she wanted to stomp a foot. "Odi!"

The nun frowned back at her. "You haven't earned that familiarity."

"And you have no idea how stubborn I can be."

The nun leaned down to the chickens then closer, onto her knees.

"My husband declared my hard-headedness a third party in our marriage."

Odile reached out to the ground. Her head hung down. Nicole realized she wasn't tossing food any more. "Odile?"

In a flash, Nicole dropped down beside her friend.

"Tired." One hand on the ground, Odile's fingers in the loose dirt. "Too much excitement."

Her eyes were tightly shut; deep wrinkles creased her forehead. "You're pale," Nicole said and felt the nun's cheek. "And cool."

Nicole yelled back to the cottage for water. Odile propped herself up on both hands, but her eyes stayed closed.

"Lean on me," Nicole said, but it was too late. The nun slumped into the dust. The chickens scattered and clucked amongst themselves.

Nicole yelled for water again and got an arm underneath Odile's waist. Light as a bag of feathers, the nun flipped into Nicole's arms without much effort. Her face had gone from cinched to placid.

"Odile!"

Her thin lips moved but not a sound.

The boy reached them first. He brought the nun's overfull pouch.

Nicole shook her, using a gentleness that matched the nun's frailty. Her body was a boneless structure. Knowing this, it seemed like a miracle that the elderly waif had pushed Nicole in the wheelbarrow at all. Maybe it was a miracle. Guilt stabbed Nicole for not having the sense to stop Odile from her determined escape plan, executed alone. Who was the most stubborn here?

Nicole steadied the nun's head while the boy squeezed drops of water into her mouth. The water covered her tongue, but she never swallowed.

"Odile," Nicole said inches from her ear. "You win. I'm not going anywhere."

The others from the cottage made it outside, and Longdac immediately knelt and listened to her chest and then to her nose and mouth. He stayed at each a long minute. Sobs welled in Nicole's throat. When he shook his head, the river of misfortune inside her overcame its banks.

PART

# 2

# PROMISE AND PERIL

# 10

# The Stakes

Two rules dominated Le Prix du Fer: participants and spectators were forbidden from speaking about it publicly, and losers couldn't leave a match alive. Everything else—odds-making, chivalry, allegiances—were a free-for-all. In many ways, the game appealed to Athos's shadowy side, the one that drank too much and disliked any constraints on the passionate ways of life. The French treasured the right to live large and dangerously. But his conscience longed for warmth and security, particularly in the arms of Nicole, whose unknown whereabouts prevented him from sleeping, resting, and eating. Staying put in Paris to await the start of Le Prix was its own definition of Hell.

Since informing Geneviève of his decision to enter, several search parties of Musketeers had returned to the city empty-handed, sinking his hopes by the minute. They'd narrowed the scope of the search but not enough. He couldn't successfully scour the remaining countryside and return in time to compete. A search on his part seemed even more futile.

Fighting still held a certain degree of appeal to Athos. Yet Camille was also right. Athos trusted Geneviève about as much as he trusted the most contemptible—the English.

And then there were the fates of Pierre and Grignan. They added another layer of complications. No word had arrived about Grignan's whereabouts either. While watching over Pierre, Athos contemplated each decision and its complexities. Time spun to a standstill.

"We'll have to keep him out of the fight somehow. Even a whiff of it, and Pierre will leap feet first. His ego is still wrapped up in chasing glory," Athos told Camille as they stared at the dozing young patient, whose sleep had become more restless with each hour.

"He can't fight, let alone sit up." Camille had continued drinking since an earlier outing. "But what if he does enter? You two could end up fighting each other. Another reason why this option is ludicrous."

"Only if we let him out of our sights."

"He could end up dead in the first round. You could, too," Camille said, snapping his fingers. "Why in God's name would you fight rather than go find her?"

"God has nothing to do with it, I assure you," Athos said, slightly distracted. He still needed to come clean about several things with Pierre. The letters from Pierre's mother were scattered across the apartment floor. Neither Athos nor Camille had felt compelled to clean up Pierre's mess.

"He didn't read them," Athos said under his breath.

Camille bent to pick one up. Athos pulled him back.

"Leave them. And leave us, I need to talk to him alone."

"Whatever you have to say to him, I should hear, too."

"It has nothing to do with Geneviève. You'd be better off searching for Grignan right now."

"So would you," Camille said.

It hammered Athos's conscience with a spike. Despite his continued worry, Athos had to make choices, and the priest would understand.

"He's the best of God's servants," Athos admitted.

Camille stood and buckled his sword to his side. "We owe him more than leaving his search to the Cardinal's men."

"If they find him, they'll be severely displeased with me for entering Le Prix."

"I think you just told me something important," Camille said, frowning, "but I haven't the vaguest notion what."

Athos relented. The information he'd left out of their earlier conversation wouldn't change his mind, but it sent Camille into a flying fit.

"You can't be serious!" Camille shot toward Athos's stiff neck. "They'll kill you? How many life-threatening pacts can one man make?"

Athos stared back. "It was just boastful talk."

"Maybe. Maybe not. But heed me," Camille went on, pointing at him, "you're one man, Athos. Not a myth, like everyone in this god-less city might think. You cannot control the fates of Pierre *and* Nicole *and* Grignan without consequences. Right now, I'd say the odds don't favour a positive outcome for one and for all."

Pierre's moaning interrupted the tirade. "No mention of Le Prix at all," Camille whispered harshly. "And don't think I'm done arguing with you about entering."

Athos moved toward him, but his friend left in a fluster.

Pierre stirred under his blanket. His face in the weak candlelight shone with a thin layer of sweat. The injuries to his hand were infecting his whole body. Athos brought a chair to the bedside and a cup of fresh water. He waited to disturb him from necessary sleep. Athos wanted him as healthy as possible, but a full recuperation would require weeks not days. He was bones and burns.

The events of the last twenty-four hours rolled around in Athos's head. Both choices—Le Prix or Nicole—contained pitfalls, and because Nicole's life teetered on Athos's cooperation one way or another, the right path was elusive. Athos wanted to trust his strength as a swordsman.

But ...

His higher-self wanted Nicole safely in his arms without delay. Not at the mercy of a vengeful woman.

Camille had been right. He needed to focus on the only path that guaranteed Nicole's safety, and that was finding her himself. Athos was better off staying out of Le Prix. With Pierre secure, for the time being, two objectives took priority—her life and the life of his son. She was so sure it would be a boy.

"Pierre," Athos said, leaning intently toward him. "It's Athos. We need to speak."

Pierre stirred again, but his eyes didn't flutter. Athos dampened a rag from Grignan's small box of cures. He laid it on one cheek and then the next. Pierre remained still.

Athos collected the loose letters from the floor and shuffled through them. His better half kept him from reading them. Nicole had exercised years of self-control by doing the same. All the understanding in the world would not change their outcome.

Pierre's breathing rattled until he developed a cough. It started weakly then grew to a harsh round of hacking. Athos brought the cup up to Pierre, who rejected the small gesture. Whatever God had in store for the young man, Athos believed any pill would be bitter to swallow.

"Don't waste your energy talking," Athos told him.

"You're still here?" Pierre eked out, his sarcasm still audible.

"Yes, I haven't left you yet. A few things kept me here. I need to tell you something."

Fading in and out, Pierre's head lolled side-to-side.

"Grignan is missing. He left to find you a doctor and didn't meet back up with us. We fear he's been captured."

Pierre blinked. Either a sign of acknowledgment or lack of energy.

"Nicole is presumed missing, as well."

The young man stopped blinking, and the muscles in his neck tightened.

"She's been abducted by the brother of the man you killed in Le Mans."

"Henri's brother? Vachon took her?" Pierre's voice was layered in phlegm.

Athos nodded. "The Musketeers are searching for her. I'm leaving to join them." He paused. "There's something else I must tell you."

"About Hannah? Baby Sophia?"

"She's fine, as far as I know, both are fine."

Pierre relaxed a little.

"Nicole is carrying my child."

The coughing returned viciously. Pierre's eyes watered, and his face soon turned splotchy and red.

Athos held the cup up to him, but Pierre knocked it away. Water sprayed the floor.

"I'm useless!" Pierre's head crushed the pillow, and he writhed. He desperately tried sealing his lips from more coughs. He spit out: "Useless!"

"Don't …"

"No!" Pierre's attempt at yelling failed. Only a harsh, hard cough came out.

"I'm confident we'll find her and Grignan. The outcome will be—"

"What? Her dead?" Pierre rasped rhetorically.

Athos got up and started for the door. "She will not die."

"You might," Pierre struggled to verbalize his anger. "Better you."

Head down, Athos took his leave and left regret behind with the angry young man.

# 11

# Twist and Turns

Nothing about Paris in the middle of the night caused Athos much pause. The rats and the cats took over the city streets. The passed-out drunks and snoring beggars littered alleys that he passed between, forging ahead toward the Musketeer headquarters. There, everything he needed to start his search for Nicole would be granted.

A few blocks from the House of Tréville, he turned a corner to find a large hooded figure in the street ahead. Moonlight provided the only illumination, and its silvery glow outlined the figure in a thin white line. It wasn't unusual to run into someone in the night, but this man wasn't moving. He stood stiller than a gargoyle on a precipice at Notre Dame.

The man stumbled forward a step. Athos stopped moving. The man had been pushed. He was still again. Then a stumble. Another push. Someone was threatening from behind. And the offender seemed intent on intimidating them both.

"Is that the Musketeer?"

The voice rang in Athos's memory. Back and forth it bounced, floundering from one murderous scene to the next. He hadn't heard the voice in almost a year, but the connection clicked and a dangerous locked passage opened.

"Vachon, show yourself."

"You surprise me," he said from behind the figure. "I guessed you'd forgotten me."

"How could I? Where's Nicole? I demand to see her and that she be released!"

Vachon pushed the large human barrier forward another step. "Don't tell me you haven't recognized this person?"

Athos squinted into the dark. The bulky outline of whomever stood between them started to take on a familiar shape. "Grignan," he murmured. No wonder the Cardinal's guards had no recollection of him among their prisoners. He hadn't made it that far.

"Let him go," Athos said and unsheathed his sword.

"Put your weapon away," Vachon admonished. He said it like a father smacking down an obstinate son. "Killing me won't get you to Nicole."

"Grignan," Athos spoke to his friend, "can you speak?"

"No, he can't," Vachon answered, "unless he can talk with a gag in his mouth. He's been through quite an ordeal. A whipping or two. His eye might require a stitch as well."

Athos lunged forward, anger whipping through him.

Vachon pulled the priest back a few steps and stood to the side, grasping the priest in one arm and aiming his sword at Athos in the other. "I wouldn't do that if I were you," he said.

Halting, Athos kept his sword drawn.

"You're doing exactly what we thought," Vachon said. "Geneviève said you'd go after her, and here you go, off in the dark of night, running for your Musketeer friends. Could you be any more predictable?"

"You wouldn't know the meaning of loyalty if it stuck you in the ass."

"Loyalty?!" Vachon manhandled Grignan into a kneeling position and re-aimed his sword. "That little waste of a man you're hiding will feel my loyalty once I get ahold of him. And I'm here to see that you make good on your promise."

Athos inched forward, calculating the speed it might take to cross twenty paces and bury his weapon in the target.

Vachon threw the hood off Grignan. The best that Athos could tell in the moonlight was that the priest had suffered a great beating about the head. His hair was matted down in spots by what must have been dried blood, and one eye was swollen shut. A taut binding stretched across his open mouth, and stuffing filled the insides. He probably hadn't the air to even grunt a note of distress.

Vachon's sword stayed at Grignan's neck.

"You will not go after her, because you won't find her. I have eyes posted at every gate around the city for you. You'll enter Le Prix as promised, or he and Nicole will die. It's that simple. This is the only warning you'll get."

Athos took another step.

"Move again and his head goes." Vachon stiffened his arm. "Next will be hers."

"And what if I don't win? There has to be another way for Nicole to survive."

"Most likely, you won't survive. Especially with me in the ring. I'm entering to increase our chances of coaxing Pierre out of hiding. He wouldn't pass up an opportunity to kill me, too. Then I can dispatch you both."

The moves and counter-moves—Le Prix, the abductions, the ultimatums—the viciousness never ended. For a brief second, the old ways of simply challenging a man to a duel seemed quaint. The edicts banning them morphed into an underground ego festival.

"Grignan," Athos said, "nod if you want me to stand down."

In the few beats that he waited for an answer, Athos's hand ached.

The priest nodded once and dropped his head to his chin and never came up. The sign of despair forced Athos to promise himself not to forget. Remembering the worst could be used for the best.

Athos lowered his sword and backed away. At the end of the street, he called to his friend, who was being forced to shuffle away, "God have mercy."

∞∞∞∞

Pierre couldn't sleep. Couldn't think. Couldn't stand the look of the four walls. The Bastille had made him hate being confined, even now in the warm bed of his friend d'Artagnan. He needed air, and he needed out.

Camille slept slumped in a chair. Silently, Pierre swung his legs to the floor and willed himself upright. A rush of blood blotted out his eyesight temporarily, and he froze to take a deep breath. He had to recover and fast. Sleeping away the majority of the past week had helped. But his mixed feelings toward the situation cornered him into an agitation that made a full recovery impossible. To recuperate, he needed space from everyone's watchful eye. Not that Paris would cooperate and open its doors to a skeletal invalid, but he wasn't making progress under Athos and his friend.

His hand and head burned. It seemed impossible to shake the heat. He collected the crucible of salve from the floor by the bed. His clothes were wilted and wrinkled from sweat. He was wholly unpresentable.

A wine bottle sat on a table near Camille. Pierre forced himself over to it and drank the last few draws. Feeling the warm liquid in his stomach recharged him. He needed to find a place to drink, eat, think, and be alone, at least until he could sort through what to do next. And that wasn't clear based on the new information.

Grignan. Gone.

Vachon. Hunting him.

Nicole. Abducted.

Athos. Off to be the hero. Again.

Pierre's dream to be a Musketeer had seemed the farthest off when he had realized he might never escape the Bastille. But being with Athos again, the loci of Musketeer lore, also dropped his hopes. Athos treated him as if he would never be good enough to be one of the elite guard. That, he decided, was intolerable. He needed to forge his way alone.

There are miracles. And then there are miraculous forces. Sometimes the two are one and the same. Tonight, force moved Pierre. He turned his back on prayer and mercy and threw himself into the arms of a city he barely knew.

∞∞∞

Athos returned to the steps of d'Artagnan's apartment after zig-zagging through the neighbourhoods for an hour. He didn't want to chance anyone following him. The early morning signs of sunrise, a pink hue above the skyline, tempted him to stay outside a while longer, but fatigue got the better of him.

He reached the top of the steps to d'Artagnan's room and barely kept his balance when he saw the door ajar. He was sure no one had followed him, but maybe his wits were elsewhere. He burst into the room and fell to Camille's side at once. Tied to the chair, his companion was stripped bare. The chair laid sideways on the floor. Camille's eyes had been closed, but he was not asleep. They popped open the instant Athos hit the floor.

"What in God's name …?" He loosened a gag in his friend's mouth.

"Pierre did this," Camille said, his jaw set in anger. "He overtook me when I was asleep."

"Are we talking about the same person? He was feverish and bed-ridden when I left."

"Something's gotten into him. But I was half-drunk and groggy as a newlywed, so my defenses were a little off. And I didn't think he was serious. At first. He wanted my clothes, so he got them, not that I cooperated much. I put up a good fight."

"Where did he go?"

"He didn't say. He just barked commands." Camille rubbed his wrists as soon as Athos cut them loose with the end of his sword.

"My night was just as unusual as yours." Athos sat on the floor as soon as Camille was up looking for clothes. "Grignan was taken by Vachon. He made sure I wasn't to leave the city and go after Nicole."

Camille shook his head as soon as he wrapped a blanket around his waist. "And Grignan?"

"Not good. Beaten to within a heartbeat of his life."

"Did you follow them?"

"I couldn't risk it." Athos clasped his hands together and beat them a few times on his forehead. "Vachon's entering Le Prix to make sure Geneviève wins and coax Pierre out into the open."

"It's everyone's fight to the death."

"There's no way out of it."

"You think there's not, but there always is," Camille said. He sat on the cot.

"We're back at the beginning."

"And the offending man-boy has gone astray." Camille fluttered his hand above his head.

Athos looked toward the small window above their heads. "He's the least of my worries. He'll be easy to track. Just follow the road to debauchery."

# 12

# The Road to Debauchery

A half hour before dark, Pierre arrived at the La Taverne du Cheval, the place he'd always associate with the story of his father. It was at the tavern that Athos had told him the real story of Remi Tremon. The man was still alive, despite Pierre's previous knowledge to the contrary.

Like his mother, his father was more of a mystery than anything else—a peasant boy who'd seduced an aristocrat's daughter. They'd run off after falling in love. The Comte ruthlessly pursued them, until Sibonne was brought home. Remi joined the gypsies as a means of survival. When Sibonne ended her life, some pact between the two lovers changed Pierre's life: without explanation, he was sent to live with Nicole, the Comtesse de Rochefort. He had been far too young to remember many details. He didn't know until recently he was secretly her nephew, hidden from society and raised as a servant. He suffered the Comte's condescension from boyhood on.

So Pierre's history entailed two insults: the mysterious abandonment by his father and the thorough disgust of his keeper. Pierre hated them both.

His stomach churned as he crossed the Rue Vieille du Temple to the tavern's front door, hoping beyond good sense that this time he'd find a benevolent benefactor. Of what kind, he didn't care.

The tavern teemed with a full range of Paris night crawlers. Men in sailing garb and servants in knickers mingled between women who liked to show more skin than fashion. A dwarf, a one-eyed man in an ancient uniform, and old beggars jostled about between tables and chairs. The servers threw ale and wine around liberally, and coins chinked from one hand or the other, switching from pockets and coin purses with the smoothness of a slinky cat.

A boisterous group in the back was drawing a crowd. Without any money to buy food or drink, Pierre decided the next best thing to do was to learn how to earn favours. He had skills, just no knowledge of how to use them outside of Rochefort or without dueling anyone.

Two men were spinning a three-sided wooden top and placing bets on which side would land up. Another man in the crowd was taking wagers. So much shouting and betting was going on at once, it was difficult for Pierre to keep track of who was making what bet and when. But that wasn't his job. His job was to get smart without looking dumb.

Across the other side of the group, several women in peasant dresses pretended not to stare at him. Off and on, he caught one of the three shooting him a sideways grin, then quickly hiding behind another so as not to arouse attention. It wasn't convincing. A large part of him appreciated the stares but couldn't fathom why anyone would find him appealing, being as skinny and beat up as he was. Maybe just being a new face caused the women to fawn. Camille's clothes were decent and clean but little else seemed worthy of attention. Luckily, the clothes hid the worst of his scrawny condition.

"You on the end, come here—boy!"

Pierre didn't bother taking notice of the barked order because "boy" didn't describe how he felt about himself anymore. He'd never be a boy again, not after surviving Hell.

"You!" The voice boomed over the crowd. A man standing by him elbowed his ribs.

Turning toward the voice, he spotted the uniformed burly frame of a guardsman of the Cardinal, craning his head right toward him. The man gave him an evil eye and took a pull off his bottle of wine. "Where did you get your sword?"

Pierre, just then, remembered he had one by his side. Camille's sword had been too great a temptation to leave behind. Few possessions meant as much as it did to a destitute loner. It hung, or rather swung, loosely from the absconded belt that badly needed a new notch for his waist.

"It's a friend's," Pierre said, the truth, if he believed he'd return it, which had been his intention.

"Then your friend won't mind if I take a quick look," the guard said.

Before Pierre could grab the sword from leaving his side, another man in the crowd swiped the weapon out of its place and tossed it over the heads in the game, mostly still engrossed in the gambling.

In his gloved hand, the guardsman caught the sword by the blade, executing a deft snap in mid-air. Pierre's teeth ground a little. He never liked a show-off.

"This is a fine piece," the guardsman said, his bushy brows moving up at each emphasized word. "Do you know how to use it?"

Finally, a way he could participate. "Of course. I've even killed a man."

The guard chuckled, as did a few others around them in the circle of hoodlums, but his laugh was tempered and turned to silence sooner than it should.

"If you've killed a man, then you must be a Musketeer."

A few more ears perked up. Pierre also didn't like to be patronized.

"You know I'm not."

"Well, you're not one of us," he said, pointing a thumb back at himself.

"I'm an apprentice."

Even more laughs rounded the circle.

"An apprentice," the guard said, an amused smirk gliding up one side of his face. "Then you know how to use this sword, if you've gotten a few lessons."

"More than a few." Pierre was enjoying the sudden attention. He'd been out of the light too long.

"You don't seem to be the fighting type."

"And what type would that be?"

"Someone with more girth to his neck."

Again, laughs circled the crowd. The gamblers were taking longer pauses between tosses to listen to the volleys above their heads.

"I have skill and something you'll never have," Pierre said.

The guard thumbed his nose and swung an arm around the group, looking for endorsement. "The boy here thinks there's something I don't have. Must be scabies."

The laughter pitched higher and *oohs* and *aahs* wound through the ranks.

"I have developed an incredible tolerance to pain." With that, Pierre removed one of his gloves, and a queer silence fell over the area. His hand—cracked, peeling, and missing the end of a pinky— symbolized unimaginable suffering.

"Tested, I see," the guard said, then exaggerated his nods at each person watching the tête-à-tête. "Well, I've also been tested."

The guard handed Pierre's weapon to a peasant and pulled his sword from his scabbard. Pierre's instincts immediately shifted to aggression at the sound of the unsheathing.

The guard flipped his weapon over once, twice. "It's almost unfair of me to duel an injured boy."

"Try me." There wasn't a bone or muscle in Pierre's aching frame that could have stopped him.

The gambling switched from a silly game of chance to a high stakes real-life duel. It was the Cardinal's Guard versus the Musketeer's Apprentice. Pierre had earned a name without even trying. And it had been accurate though he hadn't mentioned Athos was his teacher. A duel between the two known rivals, Cardinal vs. Musketeer, increased the likelihood the gamblers would bet more. The odds makers could always be counted on for exaggerated entertainment value.

"What have you got to throw in?" the odds maker asked Pierre as the group bumped and pushed toward the door.

"My life."

He wasn't worried. His hand stung, raw and red, but his predicament was having a healing effect. He was carving out his own fate, not following the good intentions of caretakers who decided for him.

"Better feed him first," called one of the mesdemoiselles who'd eyed him wantonly earlier.

"Worry about that if he survives," the burly guard said.

"You can't kill him," the odds maker told the guard. "It's too close to the tournament, and everyone is observing a moratorium on duels. There'll be consequences to pay."

"He's not going to kill me," Pierre said, poised to fight. "Besides, I have no designs on this so-called tournament."

The guard took a second look at him. This time, he spoke slower. "You don't know anything about Le Prix?"

"Shh," the odds maker said. "We're forbidden!"

"What have you got to say for yourself, boy?" The guard hoisted his sword toward him.

"I'm not a boy." Pierre lunged.

For an attack or two, the men equaled each other. The entire crowd cheered on the Cardinal's guard, not that the Cardinal himself held any favour with the masses. The guard was just a known entity. But loyalties in a street fight have the propensity to shift like fish in a shallow pool. Pierre's superior skills, though dormant for months, revived in a matter of strikes.

In the oncoming dusk, the crowd in the street grew more rowdy as Pierre took the upper hand. His clothes flapped and billowed at each charge of his opponent. The guard could defend attacks, but his weakness was offense. He wasn't able to land any good strikes, and Pierre's surges easily deflected the rudimentary technique. His winning was the most life-affirming act of independence that Pierre had experienced since … since he'd killed the Comte.

Bets changed favourites from Cardinal to Apprentice. One swift slice, and the duel would be over.

The slice came to Pierre's shirt. The loose garment slashed in two at his side, exposing the wound on his flank that sopped the bandage. A few near him drew in breaths. Pierre flailed at the loose shirt to cover himself, but the attempts were useless. The guard puzzled over the newly exposed wound.

"You're bleeding," the guard said and checked his sword for blood.

"And incredibly thin," said a peasant who was peering through two other gawking heads.

Pierre raised his sword for another attack, but the guard dodged and refused to stand *en garde*.

"Something's not right here." Pacing, the guard made the statement as much toward the crowd as to Pierre. "No one looks that bad unless…"

"Unless he's been starving," said the mademoiselle. Pierre turned to find her, curly headed and energized, right behind him. She stood as straight as the mast of a ship, an inch higher than Pierre.

"Duel over!" She stomped her foot and pulled Pierre away by the arm.

A wave of whistles and boos followed them down the street. Pierre nearly tripped a few times, confused as to why the young woman, whose clothes were a little rough around the edges, had taken up his cause.

She blew a reddish curl off her face and forced him into an alley using the strength of a mule. Out of earshot of the surly crowd, she declared, "You'll be lucky if they forget that misfitting error."

"You mean misfortunate," he said, not understanding why he was letting her drag him along or whether he'd used his last energy in one spectacular burst of pride. Her tight-fitting bodice turned his meanderings elsewhere.

"Like I said, you need to eat first."

"Why are you doing this?"

The last light and shadows of the day were disappearing into black. The alley narrowed, and she stepped high along the path. Obstacles came upon the street, things that Pierre had seen in the Bastille. Rats, piles of waste, lost souls. Even women sprawled in the streets, without proper attire or hope in their eyes. Paris was showing him another side. Or, his new intriguing companion was.

They came to a door made of ship ladder on the front of a two-story cobblestone that the city had forgotten. She knocked twice quickly, paused, and knocked twice again, not as fast. A latch clicked on the other side, and they stepped inside.

From this short passage, she relocked the door and bumped him forward, toward a warm glow through a red curtain that hung between them and the next room. Stepping through the opening, oil lamps reflected brightly from walls striped in bright yellow and pink. Nothing in his bank of memories compared. Outside his realm of experience, the colors were so garish and bold, he wanted to touch them and see if they were real. A few ratty antiques finished off the room. No other person bothered to use the parlour.

She turned and gave him a good once-over. "I can sew your shirt. The rest is up to you," she said taking a longer look at the bandage on his side. "You've been tortured, haven't you?"

He clinched his jaw and nodded.

"They'd have thrown you back in shackles if we had stuck around." She looked around the room and spotted what she wanted on a tired loveseat. It looked to be a doublet. "You can have this. Let me have your shirt."

Pierre bunched his shirtfront together, as if it were shelter and doing so fixed all his problems.

"You don't have to be modest around me. I've seen everything before." She pushed the uncooperative curl from her forehead again. He waited until she got the hint.

"All right then, food," and she disappeared through a second door covered by a black curtain.

Light-headed, Pierre flopped on the loveseat and tried to take stock. At least he wasn't at the mercy of the elements. Food was promised. A fresh, or supposedly fresh, coat laid across his lap. He pulled off his gloves and shirt. The simple act exhausted him. How could he have fought the guard and have no wherewithal to change clothes?

"I was starved once." She was back. This time she brought a bowl of broth and the end of a baguette. "I'm Jeanne, named after someone in French history with moral fortitude. Not that it carried over."

The bowl rattled on the tarnished tray as she found space next to him.

He grabbed the bread, caring little if it looked as though his manners had gone out with her knowledge of family history. "I'm Pierre," he muffled, mouth overstuffed.

"How can you not know about Le Prix?"

Pierre paused on one bite, shrugged, and continued eating, even more vigorously than before.

"Were you just let out of prison? Or did you come from the front, behind enemy lines?"

Her questions came from starry-eyed curiosity rather than concern.

"The Bastille." He attempted another sip of soup.

"No one gets out of there," she said, her nose scrunched.

"I did."

"Your hands, wrists. Scalded and shackled?"

He nodded and chewed.

"You weren't very smart to pick a fight in that condition."

He shook his head. "He provoked me. I would have killed him."

"Maybe." She surveyed his scrawny ribs, visible through the unbuttoned doublet.

"Not maybe. Definitely."

"Are you sure you don't know about Le Prix?"

"Tell me," he said and swallowed a large gulp of broth.

Her description erupted from her in one long flourish. The underground tournament occupied the hearts and minds of the Paris lower class, who loved anything they could bet on, talk secretly of, and flout as a product of their insatiable desire for distraction. Le Prix was not a venture of high society; it was a manipulation of the power of the people.

"Manifestation," Pierre corrected.

"What?" She stopped her soliloquy in mid-sentence and crossed her arms in front of her, mildly annoyed at his interruption.

"It is a 'manifestation of the power of the people,' not manipulation. Manipulation is when you get someone to do something for you but your reasons are a little secretive," he said. His bowl was empty.

"More?" She smiled at him, and for the first time, he noticed how plainly attractive she was. The color of her hair was a cross between a brown hen and a flowering quince. Her hazel eyes matched her personality: spunky.

"You remind me of a bush that bursts into scarlet in the spring time." He smiled back at her.

"And you remind me of a Musketeer."

"Anyone in particular?"

"They all have that same aloof confidence. You have it. You should enter."

"The tournament? What for?" He glanced at the bandage around his side. He was nowhere near healed.

"Wait," she said and disappeared, tray in hand.

A few heavier footsteps in the back room told him they were not alone.

She arrived back at his side carrying another bowl of soup and a clean rag. She nodded for him to let her do it. The old bandage unwound quickly and both grimaced at the open wound.

"What happened?" she said as she started redressing it.

"A mistake."

"Must have been a bad one."

"More than you'll ever know." Another noise came from the back. The room suddenly got smaller, a little less safe. "Do you live here?"

"I stay here."

"All the time?"

"Most of the time."

"And what do you do here?"

Laughter floated down from the rafters above them. He looked up. She tied the bandage in place.

"Save men from themselves." And she pulled him into a kiss.

∞∞∞

Just as Jeanne had not grasped the concept of manipulation, Pierre had never fully gathered the meaning of brothel. Jeanne was definitely not his idea of a whore. She smelled good, tasted good, loved him good.

After the first time, he immediately said a prayer for forgiveness. His love for Hannah never came into question. Feeling better about himself, he immediately fell asleep, somewhere upstairs in the chambers where she had taken him. It was a journey of blind turns, whispered touches, and the smells of musk and copulation. Hues of deep reds and purples. Behind doors, the muffled talk of women and men drifted in. The jostling of bodies under sheets and on soft surfaces. The place shocked and titillated him. How could he have not given in to her?

The second time they did it, after a slumber so long he wasn't sure what time of day it was or whether he'd slept more than a day, he felt less guilty. He skipped the prayer. He enjoyed the freedom to take what was offered and not ask too many questions of his morals.

One leg was thrown over her. "You're named after Jeanne d'Albret of Navarre. She was a champion for the French Huguenots."

"A nun?" Jeanne said, squirming her naked body against his in a toying manner.

"Oh no. She was a Calvinist," he said and kissed her sloppily on the cheek. "You're a queen and the mother of a king."

"Queen Jeanne!" she raised a fist and laughed at herself.

He held her tighter and admired her firm breasts, the only other set of breasts he'd ever had permission to kiss his entire life.

"How do you know so much?" Her indirect compliment caused his strength to return for round number three. The romp was hardly long enough to break the thread of their conversation.

She blew a stray curl from her face. "You aren't a peasant, are you?"

"I am, and I'm not."

"You talk in circles."

"And I kiss in them, too."

He started on her temple, moved to cheek, then chin, and stopped at her glistening forehead.

"You're also not a virgin," she said.

"If I had been, I'm not now."

"Who is she?"

Pierre twisted a red curl on his finger. An infinitesimal pang of regret beat inside him. "I haven't seen her in almost a year." Could it be? He might not even recognize his daughter.

"That's what happens to us, the people they throw away," she said and sat up. Her naked body cured his regret.

"Now my turn for an inquisition," he said and wiggled so that she straddled the only part of him that didn't hurt, his groin. "Why have you decided to help me? I'm quite self-sufficient."

Her breasts bounced with her laughter.

"All right, all right, so I could stand a little help. But, why me?"

"You aren't like the other men who want to duel."

"Of course, I'm half their age."

"How old are you?" She leaned her front onto his chest.

Seventeen, well, not anymore. "I spent my eighteenth birthday in chains."

"Why were you there?"

"I'm supposed to be asking the questions," he said and put a finger to her lips. "Aren't you entitled to require something from me in exchange for this?"

She looked him up and down. "Not the ones who have potential."

This time, he launched into a short fit of laughter. "Me?" he asked. "Potential?"

"You have no fear and a high tolerance for pain. You said so, out in the street."

He nodded but kept it short. He noticed a starry-eyed glint in her smile.

"Then you must enter Le Prix."

"I have absolutely no strength to go round after round. Maybe with you," he said, offering a kiss. "But not in the ring. Even I'm not that stupid."

Her smile widened. "The winner of Le Prix earns status and fortune. He becomes a legend."

"Why haven't I heard of it before?"

"We're not supposed to talk of it in public, but the last winner walked away as flush as a duke. No one touched him or challenged his new status, at least for a while."

"What happened to him?"

"Beheaded by the Cardinal."

Such is the fate of infamous men, thought Pierre. "How much money?"

"It depends on how much is wagered. The cut is 70/40, the better part going to the winner. The rest, to the men who risk organizing it."

A duke's wealth for a duel. He couldn't say he wasn't intrigued. "You helped me," he said, pushing up on his elbows, kissing distance from one perfect taut bud, "because you think I can win and you'd take some of the winnings."

Her smile grew into a sunburst. The strings attached to her weren't without their benefits. His mouth nabbed a nipple and nipped it between his teeth.

"Hey!" She pulled back and squeezed her chest.

"If I am to enter Le Prix, I'll have to eat something more than you and soup."

# 13

# Reconciliation

Distraught, Athos clung only to hope. The hunt for Nicole had slipped through his fingers. Their enemies had caged him. Out in the streets, he was merely a target, too.

With two days left before the last fight of his life, he cordoned himself off in a corner of the Musketeer base, awaiting anyone's return from the mission to save her. Few were left in the field. At any small noise near the entrance, his nerves jumped and he pounced on whomever entered the yard. His incessant watch at the front gate drove many of the guardsmen to stop using it to come and go.

Trèville, who rarely kept a strict headcount of his Musketeers, joined Athos at a small table late one night, drinks in hand. Athos refused.

"You're driving us all to drink when you're usually the one out-drinking us all," Trèville said.

"It's useless. I'm chained like a beast."

"If my men find Vachon, which is our best hope, all of this will be over."

"I've underestimated him." Athos dug a thumbnail into the wood. "And Geneviève."

"A royal bitch," Trèville said and took a drink. "She's so far up the rank, unless we caught her holding a bloody sword, she could get away with assassination."

"I've killed women before," Athos said.

Trèville gripped him by the forearm. "This is different. She's not a branded woman."

Athos, though sober, took that memory out of hiding for a moment, a rare occurrence. "Women have perpetuated more evil in my life than the worst of men."

"Yet, you love one." Trèville got up to leave. "Don't go dark on us again."

"It's time."

Trèville puzzled over the statement.

"I need to leave the guard. If I make it through the next few days and Nicole survives, I'm returning to my sovereignty and staying out of this place." He gave the familiar surroundings a stern appraisal.

"In this case, I agree," Trèville said, and without ceremony, left.

Athos had expected an argument, but in the scheme of things, it mattered only whether he could live to see the plan through.

Minutes later, Camille ran through the gate, disturbing the relative quiet.

"There's news of Grignan."

Athos met him in the middle of the yard. "He's found?"

"No, but another priest remembers seeing someone who resembled him in the neighbourhoods around Notre Dame. He wasn't alone. But it was several days ago."

"That makes sense," Athos said. "If Vachon goes through with Le Prix, he'll want to keep Grignan as close to him as possible. Did you go to the Place de Grève?"

"It's as quiet as a chapel. The peasants have viciously sealed their lips about the tournament. Even the shopkeepers deny anything is going on."

Preoccupied in thought, Athos strode to the gate and back, conjuring any detail he could from that dark night Vachon had approached him with the beaten Grignan. It would have taken a pack of horses to disturb his thoughts, and that's what finally did.

Three Musketeers on horseback flew through the gate and rounded the yard in record speed. A rallying cry circled the compound. On one horse, Nicole clung to the back of Longdac, an elated hero.

Athos spilled toward her and had her off the horse and into his arms as if it were the only job his body was designed to do. He enveloped her in a tidal wave of care. He uttered incoherent words of thanksgiving and couldn't conceive she was not a vision.

"I'm real, Athos. Real. In one piece."

A flurry of congratulations rounded the men who brought her to him, though Athos was too engrossed in keeping her close to join in.

"This is my fault," he told her, more than once.

"Don't say that. Just breathe and take me somewhere to rest, no noise."

Before the words came out of her mouth, he started moving them away to a small weapons room. The celebration behind them continued on, and wine arrived.

In the quiet, he could breathe again. Everything he could give thanks for suddenly stood within reach. She allowed several passionate kisses until he understood the depth of her fatigue. He was holding her up, and capable though he was, she turned limp in his embrace. She had fainted.

"Water!" Athos shouted toward the outdoors, and the din of the celebration drowned him out. "Water, by God! She's gone under!"

Another loud moment passed before someone in the periphery calmed the group, and men instantly sprung into motion. The little room promptly filled with provisions for nursing the near-dead. Water and rags and basins and tonics. Without a bed or flat surface to place her, Athos ordered the men to bring a bench in, where he laid her down as gently as thin glass.

He sent men for a doctor and brandy. Someone suggested a midwife. He stayed by her, clasping her hands, waiting for her re-emergence. An old wise woman, who was summoned from a nearby nunnery, showed up faster than was possible, for her age.

"I ran her here on my back," Longdac said, puffing, and excused himself.

Everyone but Athos and the woman exited the room.

She worked her way from head to ankles. Athos whispered in Nicole's ear, hoping his prayers might revive her.

"Exhaustion." The woman crossed herself and prepared a tonic in a cup. Directing Athos to hold her head up, the old woman slowly drained the liquid into Nicole's mouth. Her listlessness didn't change.

"My love," Athos said. His lips felt at home on her neck, nearest the strongest heartbeat. He watched the faint tic, the surest clue to her wellness.

The woman prepared a second tonic. "Give this to her in an hour. She'll be sleepy. Keep her in bed." The woman felt Nicole's belly again. "Don't move her too much, just make her more comfortable."

Then the woman was gone.

The quiet—and a second wave of heavy accountability—swallowed him in one swoop.

He quickly gathered a few men to transport her to her home in the Montmartre quarter. She hadn't been in her Paris residence since mourning the Comte's death, but it was the only place for her. Full of lush furnishings and the finest linens, her bedroom, once the chamber for her and her husband, transformed into a place of recovery.

Athos asked Longdac to keep guard at the front door and arrange for a replacement every three hours. As long as Pierre was missing, she was still a potential target. Her rescue shed light on several developments: why Vachon had kidnapped Grignan and why Geneviève was so obsessed with capturing Pierre.

He waited and watched for any movement of her recovery. He bottled up every question he held about her ordeal. He could only marvel at her strength. Her condition had not affected her beauty. It heightened it. He experienced greater appreciation for her. Love in expanse. His hands stayed on hers, and he hoped they'd work as a magnet for the hurt and confusion. How unfair for her to bear Vachon and his ill-treatment, on top of the layers of pain and complexity she had already overcome. Another lashing onto a scar.

A few hours before dawn, she rustled. Her eyes fluttered but fell shut. The struggle was easier to forgo, and Athos prepared a wet rag. He laid it on a cheek and took encouragement that her body was unharmed. Her mind, yet to be determined.

The damp rag on her face lit a small light in her. She blinked to attention and squeezed his hands. "I've finally made it."

"I love you."

She squeezed again. "And I, you."

Athos took a deep lungful of air and gave his body permission to stand down. "I feel deeply responsible for this abominable turn of events."

It wasn't necessary, but he shouldered the blame.

"Vachon told me he was going to use me to hurt you and Pierre."

"He's not working alone," Athos said, leaning closer. "A woman you may know is part of the plot."

"Geneviève de Montpensier."

Athos took her hands and planted several kisses on them. Whatever it took to improve the outlook, he'd try.

"Athos," she said, urging him to look up. "I've known about her and my husband for many years. You don't have to bandage that wound."

"I'm worried she'll come for you again. I have men at the door. They'll stay night and day. Trèville has sent Musketeers across the city to apprehend Vachon. He's elusive." He didn't want her to look away. "Tell me what happened."

"You'll either be proud of me or incredibly aggravated. I escaped."

His short laugh covered up his concern. "Your fugitive days should be behind you."

"I hid in a church. An old nun cared for me and took me to safety until the Musketeers found us."

Athos heard a sadder tone in her voice. "What happened that you aren't telling me?"

"She died." Her voice shook. "She used the last hours of her life, her last energy, to save me."

Athos smoothed her hair flat on the pillow. Her tears fell and disappeared between the strands.

"We buried her in a cemetery by the church. It wasn't a proper burial because the priest was too drunk to give the sacrament."

Athos offered her water. She took a long drink and drifted toward another deep thought.

"How do you feel?" He wasn't so much asking as attempting to distract her from a dark door.

"So very tired."

"And the baby? He grows." The firm rise beneath his hand gave him promise, hope.

"He reminds me to eat."

The remark jogged Athos out of the conversation and to his first duty, nursing her back to normal. He brought a tray of fruit and cheese to her side. After several bites, a bit of colour returned to her cheeks.

"I want to know about Pierre," she said.

He offered her a pinch of bread and shook his head no until she ate it. He hadn't decided how much to tell her or where to begin.

"He's no longer in the Bastille," he said, but had to gently push her back onto the pillow to temper her excitement. "But he isn't under my care."

"Where is he then?"

"Camille and I took him to d'Artagnan's apartment on the Rue du Vieux Colombier after his release. It was safer than taking him to my quarters in the Rue Férou. But Pierre got away from us several days ago. He's angry about his situation."

"Angry? But you freed him."

Athos gave her another bite of bread. "Grignan got him out."

"God bless Grignan! Our letters worked!"

Athos almost went along with the misconception, telling her what she wanted to hear.

"No, he never read any of our letters. Grignan took it upon himself to plan a rescue. We saw to it that it didn't end up badly."

"But our letters …"

"He never got the letters. He had to go into hiding. Rumours began to circulate that he was implicated in the Comte's death. So, he hid and concocted a way to get Pierre out of that purgatory. We arrived at the right time because they were caught during the escape. They were to be sent to Prague."

"I must thank him. We must tell him he's done God's work."

"I already have."

She settled back, taking a moment to absorb the news she'd prayed about for months.

Despite her fatigue, her wits stayed focused. "Why is Pierre so angry that he would leave you?"

Athos counted a hundred other questions he would have rather answered. "He thinks I abandoned him."

"I or we?" she completed his thought. "But we did not ..."

He guided her back down and plumped her pillow. "No, we did not abandon him, but he was confined for almost ten months. When a man spends that much time alone and in fear of his life, his thoughts contort."

"I love him," she said, a quiet admission.

"He'll forgive."

The light of dawn started to creep into the bedroom window. It reminded Athos of better times. "I'll never forget our first night together. It changed me. One night."

She brought his hands to her cheek, and her heavy lids fell to half-closed. The conversation was over, for the time being.

# 14

# The Spark

Not a man nor woman in the underbelly of Paris spoke of Le Prix in the context of daily life. In their brief excursions outside the brothel, Pierre and Jeanne tended to their survival on the same level as the wretched, the ill, the broken, and deformed. They became the criminal and the whore.

Grungy markets, miserly shopkeepers, and petty thieves were obstacles to be maneuvered around to procure food and provisions. Before each trip, Jeanne left Pierre alone in her room for short intervals and arrived back with a few pistoles to spend on their nourishment. He didn't ask details.

But there was a charge in the air. The tournament in the catacombs below the Cathedral at Notre Dame would start in two nights, and the electrifying anticipation made the hungry more rabid, the bawdy more vulgar, the young and arrogant inflamed by grandiose dreams.

Every young peasant's dream was to win Le Prix. Pierre decided to be their champion.

"We don't have enough money," Jeanne said on one of their short outings.

Pierre was sniffing an over-ripe plum. "Not even for this?"

"To enter you into the tournament," she said but kept the last part to a low whisper.

He put the plum down, and the fruit merchant moved it out of his reach. "You didn't tell me we had to pay to enter."

"Everyone does."

"How much?"

"Four hundred pistoles."

Pierre gagged on his bite of a stolen fig.

"But I have an idea," she said and marched them through the streets on a mission.

They ventured through austere lanes and past aging buildings, both towering and stout, that created a patchwork of architectural patterns along the streetscape. Pierre envisioned a spot so high in the city that he could see his countryland.

"There is such a place," Jeanne answered him and pointed toward Notre Dame. "The summit of the towers."

"Can it be climbed?"

"By the determined, of course."

They turned down a sharp corner and came to a jumble of small shops. Among the skinny facades, they arrived at a storefront with a bright red door. She rang a tasseled bell and waited. Ten, twenty seconds. A higher-pitched bell rang inside, and she responded by ringing again.

A short woman attended the door. "Are you the King of Clubs or the Queen of Hearts?"

"Neither," Jeanne responded.

The woman opened the door and led them into a tight vestibule. She left after informing them they'd be retrieved by the Jack of Spades.

"Where are we?" Pierre asked as soon as the woman disappeared.

"The gambling houses of Rue de Glatigny."

"There's more than one?"

"It's better not to ask."

Though several shades different than his, Jeanne's education had its own value. But on the other hand—"I thought we had no money. Gambling requires money."

She spun him around to be met by their escort. The man's coat was appliquéd with small red spades. Jack had arrived.

The pathway through the house spun Pierre's mind. Whoever had laid out the Bastille must have also planned the gambling house. He lost his sense of direction within the first three turns. Jeanne, always the light-hearted jester, danced her way through.

At the last door, Jack stated he went no further. Jeanne forged ahead.

On the other side of the door, they overlooked a hall that opened up to a room larger than most parlours. On a tight landing, Jeanne and Pierre stood above a crowd that congregated down a short flight of steps. People collected in pockets of a dozen or so at as many tables. The laughter and the wine flowed freely. Pierre identified several games he knew—cards, dice— and drew a blank on the rest.

Before Jeanne got away from him on the steps, he grabbed her hand and probed again. "I thought we had no money."

"Yes, but you have other things we can gamble."

"Such as?"

"Do you want to enter Le Prix or not?"

Pierre believed in her smarts about this adventure, but he'd never placed his faith in anyone for too long, not even Nicole. His silence settled it.

They wandered from group to group absorbing the games and the people playing them. Mostly men, the gamblers played for small pots, worth a few bottles of good wine or a night at an inn; but there were a few in huddles, which Jeanne gravitated to, who played for much higher stakes. The gamblers ranged from men who wore expensive embroidered silk ties and another set who could barely disguise their darting glances of desperation. Pierre checked his nervousness to make sure he wasn't doing the same.

A group of five men playing a high stakes game of rummy interested Jeanne the most. At the end of a series of hands, when many of the players started complaining about losses, Jeanne faked a whisper into one of the men's ears. On purpose, her proposition was loud enough for the men to hear.

"How would you like something more interesting to bet on?"

An eyebrow was raised by everyone, even the spectators.

"You don't have a penny to your name," a mustached fellow among the card players said. His brush-off had the opposite effect of discouraging her. She took up the role of master of the ribaldry.

"My lords, this man," she said and shoved Pierre front-most, "has a very peculiar ability."

"If his choice of women is the peculiarity, we're not interested," the mustached man said. The group snickered. Pierre frowned that the joke was at their expense and shot Jeanne an aggrieved glance.

Running her hands from the top of his head to his boots, she declared, "He cannot feel pain."

The jovial hoots and hollers enlarged her showmanship. She clicked her heels and twirled Pierre around twice. The second time, he seethed upon passing her: "A little much, don't you think?"

Someone barked at them, "He's hardly a man!"

"You're a joker," another blustered.

"I'll take that!" she said. "The joker is always the wild card."

The laughter leaned in her favour. Until she undid the bandage on his missing digit. A hush fell over the gamesmen.

"So we inflict some pain upon him," said the man with the mustache, "and if he flinches or cries out, he loses and we win. Is that the game?" He looked at her. "But you've got nothing to bet."

"Not quite what I had in mind," she said and leaned closer to the playing table. "You wager against each other and place bets on what his reaction will be. Anything counts. If he jerks or winces, you win. If he moans, you win. If he squalls, you win. If he runs around like a headless chicken ..."

"We win!" the group shouted.

"Whoever among you is closest to guessing the outcome, wins the pot, and we win nothing. But if my friend succeeds and takes the pain for at least a minute, we take all!"

A flurry of conversations and arguments erupted among the gamblers and spectators. Pierre took Jeanne aside, trying to fathom the trouble she'd just gotten him into. "This is ludicrous and bound to put me in worse shape than I'm in now."

She kissed him. "I have faith in you!"

She stepped back up to the group and savoured her handiwork. The men were negotiating as if their entire fortunes hinged on the bet. The mustached man led the chaos, a sure sign Jeanne's tactics had worked. Pierre raced through a dozen possible scenarios: a lost limb, a severed tongue, a blackened eye. These men, roused by the possibility of a new sport, would not let him off easily.

"Here, here!" the man with the mustache shouted and beat the heel of a boot on the table, not his own, mind you.

"First," Jeanne interrupted, "we must negotiate the injury."

Many of the men nodded.

"It cannot be deadly, nothing that will cause him to die. That's not a fair wager. It also must not affect his speech, his sight, or his hearing. Those cannot be replaced."

"I say a thumb," the man with the mustache said.

"A thumb can't be replaced!" Pierre couldn't help it. His verbal outburst caused a round of betting to begin, mostly because those betting thought he would cry like a baby if a digit flew off.

Jeanne backed him up from the crowd and patted his chest. "Let me handle this."

She turned back to the group. "My friend needs both his thumbs to participate in Le Prix."

The betting ground to a halt, mainly because she mentioned the contest by name. Several in the group grew wide-eyed and turned their heads to the room to see if anyone else had overheard. Speaking of the secret could get them tortured.

"This so-called Prix," the man with the mustache said, hedging, "is only for the greatest swordfighters. Is this man a great swordfighter?"

"He's a Musketeer's apprentice."

Again, the betting swelled to a high pitch. Pierre's stomach ached, a bad omen. His thumb might be the sacrificial lamb.

"If not the thumb, then the other pinky," said another gambler.

Many in the group nodded.

"Who'll do the honours?" the mustache asked.

Murmurs circled around the table. No one, not even Pierre, had a sword or knife. Maybe he would be spared, but he recognized the futility of that idea. That ship had left port.

The Jack of Spades stuck his head into the scene. In his possession: a clean butcher knife. He shrugged at the quizzical stares. "Never know when you'll need one."

Final bets were cast, and the money was held by a bet-keeper. The amount of the pot was just shy of the entrance fee to Le Prix.

Pierre took his place at an opening cleared for him at the table. There was no running from this fate, and he refocused on the truth that Jeanne had so entertainingly bandied about: that he could endure any pain. Given the reasons why he'd developed the tolerance, the end of a finger seemed a small sacrifice for glory.

In the clothes borrowed from Camille, Pierre smoothed the wrinkles out of the doublet and placed his left hand, palm down, on the wooden tabletop, fingers as wide as they would spread. The circle of people around him widened, and the hum of gamblers in the parlour quieted to a soft lull. Most of the faces in the room blazed on him and the pending act of brutality. Eyes darted from his finger to Pierre's attitude.

*This is insane.* But he gave Jeanne credit for her ingenuity. Success here could earn him two things: money to enter Le Prix and a reputation as a force to be reckoned with.

"I'd prefer you chop only once," he told the Jack of Spades.

He looked around, tried not to gulp too loudly, and nodded okay.

A collective inhale seized the crowd. Pierre locked eyes with the man who'd bet heavily against him, the man with the mustache.

The swoosh of the knife reminded Pierre of a horse that had stomped on his hand once while cleaning a stall. That pain was the most excruciating of his young life.

The blade thwacked the wood. A second passed before the shock of the severing struck his nerves. A stinging surge jolted up his arm and screamed danger to every cell of his body. His eyes stayed focused on the man with the mustache, who's mouth dropped more sourly with each passing click that Pierre stayed quiet.

For what seemed like more than a minute, not a man in the house questioned his fortitude. Jeanne squealed with joy as she counted 48, 49, 50 … in a growing tremour. It was the last Pierre heard before he passed out.

∞∞∞

"Four-hundred pistoles?!" Camille blurted.

Athos drummed his fingers on a desk downstairs in Nicole's library.

Camille shook his head and stared out a window. The sun had started to fade. "You're going to have to tell her then. It's the only way to get the money together in time. The tournament starts tomorrow."

"I'd rather not."

"She'll pay it whole-heartedly if she thinks it will save Pierre's life. You have to win so he doesn't get killed."

"We don't know if he'll even enter. And I can't guarantee anyone won't kill him."

"But you could win and spare him in the process."

Athos felt less certain of that outcome. "Now that I have Nicole safely back and Pierre is free, there's no immediate threat to their lives. Geneviève and Vachon have neither of them. We've won."

"Except for Grignan and Pierre's unpredictable nature. If he enters, you have to be prepared, even if it means you forfeit." Camille took a letter opener from the desktop and jabbed it into the soil of a nearby potted plant. "The other unknown is what Geneviève thinks happened to Nicole. They know she's disappeared, but they don't know that you have her, safe and sound. So if you don't enter, you'll tip them off."

"Less than forty-eight hours ago you were telling me to run for the hills."

Camille sighed in agreement. "This is the most tormenting set of circumstances I've ever known. It makes working for the Comte seem like a nursery rhyme."

"She won't approve of Le Prix. It's the very thing she despises about Court, superficial gamesmanship," Athos said.

"That's not the only reason why she won't like it."

Camille was right. Athos couldn't participate in a single round of deadly duels without each slash having the potential to crush her. And kill him.

"We need a backup plan," Camille redirected. "Chances are Pierre hasn't the strength to fight. Most likely, he's passed out drunk or cavorting with God knows whom." Camille chuckled, a wild look of reminiscence on his face.

"Yes, let's hope."

∞ ∞ ∞

Pierre's head ached behind his eyes, closed and dreamless. The throbbing pain in his forehead and temples was a secondary consequence. His hand pulsated angrily in dull time to each hard beat in his skull. His eyes flashed open to a murky room, a single candle, and Jeanne asleep in an armchair.

He didn't recognize the place. It wasn't her room in the Beaubourg quarter. This room was smaller, browner, plainer. The cot was made for one. Was he the patient or the condemned?

Wincing back the headache, he attempted to sit up but couldn't grasp the side of the bed. Bandages wrapped around his entire left hand and doubled its size. In addition to its girth, his hand seemed to weigh more than a blacksmith's iron. At least there was no signs of blood.

He put the pieces of his last coherent memories together, or at least the last hour. His last recollection was the gambling parlour, an abrasive shock, and then dark closing in. He'd shrunk into a tunnel that removed the pain.

And, despite what Jeanne had proclaimed, he had felt every last tinge of it.

He tried his voice, but it cracked from dryness. Even his saliva seemed gone. He experienced a strange urge to untie the bandages on his hand and view the damage himself. He hadn't looked when the knife came down nor afterward, when it took every speck of his wherewithal to force the pain out of his body and mind for a short while. Still, he'd fallen. His head pressed heavily into the pillow, and the bump on the back ached.

Jeanne fluttered awake to half-witted attention. She yawned wider than a pomegranate. Maybe the quiet and rest had done them good.

She inched the chair over to his bedside. "Better?"

He used his right hand to scratch under the bandages. "My hand is a club." He raised it and swung, but not very far. She laughed at his joke. She caught the arm and placed it gently across his ribs.

He couldn't recall if they'd won. He burrowed into the sheets. "So, there goes our chances for Le Prix."

Her jovial mood wasn't fazed. "No, you didn't win. But we have ourselves a benefactor."

*A benefactor?* "Are there such things?"

"Oh, quite." She said fluffing her hair and licking down a wiry eyebrow that had gone rogue during her nap.

"Someone will pay for me to duel?"

"Of course." The smile, the curly red hair, the persistent optimism. She laid the world at Pierre's feet.

"And this resulted from my poor showing?"

"Poor? You stood for almost a minute before reality hit you. A statue of Magellan, you were." Her eyes shimmered.

"Michelangelo."

"Who?"

"Never mind," he said and waited for the rest of the story.

# 15

# The Eve of Le Prix

Because Parisians loved a good drama, the theatrics leading up to Le Prix de Iron lived up to expectation. Athos, usually the last Musketeer to be convinced of a far-fetched story, believed few of the rumours. One story went that pigeons dropped stones wrapped in notes from the rooftops to announce the game. Another tale involved messages written in oil slicks on the Seine, which indicated when and how the contest was to be played. Because none of the peasants dared to speak, Athos doubted every story about the tournament, especially the price to enter.

All skepticism aside, anticipation ripened about the event. Some signal—the clang of a bell or blast of a cannon—seemed imminent to announce the start. Athos sat quietly in Nicole's bedroom, a sanctuary for his unease.

"Sit by me," Nicole urged, up from a light sleep.

Like the night before, Athos took a place on the bed so he could rub her back. She moved her body a little at each touch to indicate the best places for his hands. He read the subtle body cues to mean her strength was returning.

Their closeness made his next conversation more difficult to start.

"What do you know of this woman, Geneviève?" he asked.

"Very little," she said, becoming still.

"She cannot know you've arrived in Paris. If she does, she may come for you."

"Does she know Pierre is free?"

"She does, and also that I no longer have control of him. She and Vachon won't stop until Pierre is dead."

Athos felt a slight shudder run up her. He kissed her bare nape just above the nightshirt.

"I'd like to see Pierre and Grignan before we leave Paris," she told him. "I cannot force Pierre to be under my wing any longer. He's a grown man, whom I hope will return to his rightful place in Rochefort. But I cannot impose that on him."

"There are complications."

She took his hand. "I'm beginning to think we'll never outrun them."

The comment sunk his confidence. "We're together. Little else matters to me."

She rolled onto her back. He took this as a sign to rub her belly, but she kept his hand still. "I need for our life to be normal. I've lived far too many years in a state of disharmony. We must transcend this turmoil. I keep asking myself, what does that mean? I cannot live in chaos, Athos."

"All we can do is hope."

"We don't seem to do that well either," Nicole said, a blankness in her gaze.

Athos took a long pause before pressing on with the bad news. "Grignan is being held by Vachon. I fear if I don't do as they ask, they'll kill him."

Athos didn't give her a moment. "They want me to enter a sword match, Le Prix du Fer. If I win, Grignan's life will be spared."

"A game of swords? Athos ..." A wrinkle formed between her brows.

"And because I let Pierre get away, Vachon is entering to coax him out of hiding. If I enter, I could spare his life, too."

He needed to say the last piece of the puzzle. "They don't know you're safe, Nicole. If I don't enter the games, if we leave Paris, they'll know."

Nicole's calm faded with each passing revelation. "Here we are again. Trouble at every turn."

"I believe the games start tonight. I just need to make a showing."

Her tone hardened. "It plays right into what they want. Maybe Grignan got away, like I did. Maybe Pierre won't enter."

"I saw Vachon with Grignan. He confronted me the night you arrived."

"Tell me ..."

"Vachon is not backing down. He's ruthless. Trèville has poured Musketeers into the city to find him. They've turned up nothing."

She closed her eyes contemplatively. "Le Prix is a dueling competition. I remember hearing about it. I thought it was gossip or a fable to keep the peasants entertained." Her breath caught. "No one lives but the winner."

He sat up and gathered her close. He cherished that her love always radiated toward him. "You know that I'm the surest of men with my sword. Right now, we have few other advantages. I could save them both."

"Pierre might not enter." But the truth deflated her. "You could be pitted against him."

Athos curled his fingers around hers. "If so, I'd forfeit. You're my champion, Nicole. I fight for you."

Her crumbling spirit didn't care. Tears moistened her lashes. "I just want the chaos to end."

A flurry of knocks at her bedroom door interrupted their embrace. Camille cried out from the other side.

"Athos! Paris is burning! Le Prix is afoot!"

∞∞∞

As soon as Athos departed, Nicole's ire for Geneviève replaced her worry. She rose from bed and dressed in her finest day gown and jacket. The high waist gave the baby ample room. In her wardrobe mirror, she took a serious assessment of herself. The ermine trim and beige silk sleeves set off the olive tones in her complexion. The custom-tailored gown and smart jacket solidified her position of extreme wealth, the kind of status she was capable of living, if she chose to pursue a life at Court. The point was to play the part, in extremis.

She found her matching gloves and Italian calfskin shoes. As she took the stairs, she practiced straightening her back so that her poise reflected an air of self-importance. A few steps from the bottom, Longdac left his post by the front door and took several steps toward her before he shook himself from a daze.

"Madame!" he declared and bowed.

"I need a coach and an escort. I have an important visit to make."

The trip took them through the finest neighbourhoods in Paris, where news of Le Prix meant little. Aristocrats tended to bunch together, and Nicole's home was in a most exclusive section. Where they drove was also reserved for the most wealthy, but Geneviève's accommodations were slightly less affluent than Nicole's. For a noble, the differences were small but obvious. Fewer flourishes on exterior stonework, less prominent iron door-knockers, a lack of a third layer of silk sheers on the window coverings. Nicole noted the subtleties to bolster her confidence a fraction. Any superiority in this game could help remove Geneviève from her life.

Nicole did not despise her. Simply pitied her. The finest of men and women in French society always watched their backs and worried about position. Allegiances and counter-allegiances replaced life's simpler pleasures—good company, fine food, the arts. Those higher pursuits were part of aristocratic life in Paris but were often used as tools to build reputations and secure favours. Many times, the mechanizations turned ugly and foul. It wasn't entirely Geneviève's fault that she had evolved into the hateful creature who threatened Nicole and her closest circle.

At Geneviève's cobblestone entrance, Nicole sent Longdac to announce her arrival. She wasn't going in; Geneviève had to come out. Nicole wanted the meeting on her terms and under the protective watch of a Musketeer.

From the carriage window, Nicole concluded that her first tactic—not to step foot in the household—succeeded. Geneviève carried herself to the coach steps, overburdened by a boulder of pride on her shoulders. A scythe couldn't have pried open Geneviève's locked jaw.

Longdac barred her from the door, his forearm almost pressing into her tightly bound bosom. "Before you enter," he said, "I must ask you to disarm."

The comment met an arrow of poison from the noblewoman. Geneviève ground herself into the cobblestone. Her tongue lashed back. "Your ridiculous concern is unwarranted. Stand aside. I'm the one being beckoned."

Longdac's frown deepened. "Mademoiselle, one strange hiccup from the coach, and I will be at your throat." Then he stepped back and opened the door.

Nicole had dealt with worse. Her husband had trained her well. Situated in the opposite seat, Geneviève smiled at her from a place of renowned contempt.

"I would have thought you dead," Geneviève started.

"Isn't that what you wanted?"

The crinkles in Geneviève's skirt sounded like kindling on fire. "If that is what I had wanted, you would be dead by now."

Nicole held Geneviève's smile for a moment, strained by the disbelief that a woman could embrace evil so easily. Where had goodness run afoul?

"I'm not here to seek retribution for your actions against me," Nicole said. "I'm here to strike an agreement."

Geneviève blurted *ha*. "You have nothing to bargain with. You don't have control over Pierre, and we have Grignan. What do you have that I want?"

"This." Nicole ran her hands through the fur trim on her coat and across the velvet seats of the coach. "Everything you were denied. You wanted more than anything to be the Comtesse, to live the life of extreme privilege. But my husband denied you. Preferred me over you." Nicole forced herself to let the insult settle in before continuing. "But you could be here now, and no one would stand against it."

Geneviève's jaw tightened. "You never deserved him."

Nicole leaned over and touched Geneviève's knee. She instantly recoiled. "I didn't want him. And now I simply want to be left alone. You can have everything, if you leave me in peace."

"That's impossible. You're the rightful heir."

"Nothing is impossible," Nicole said determinedly.

"Your wealth and title are secure. The thought of simply handing them over to me is pure madness. You're insane."

"No. Quite the opposite." Nicole shook her head. "You've cornered me. I'm using what I have. It's everything I have, and it's undeniably sweet." Glancing around the interior, Nicole saw every envious reason to want it. Luxury, grandeur, perfection. But it wasn't perfect. That realization had taken years to see.

"Everything? You're giving me everything? Including the title Comtesse de Rochefort?"

"Including the title. But you and Vachon must never harm Pierre. You must swear to release Grignan as soon as possible and leave me and my servants and family alone in perpetuity. This includes Athos."

"And," Geneviève said, one eyebrow up, staring at Nicole's belly, "your progeny."

She covered her middle with her hands and nodded.

"You're denying your future heirs wealth and privilege. You've never lived without either. You'll face ridicule, shame." Geneviève's face shined with smug victory.

"Yes. Struggle," Nicole said. She might learn a radically different kind of life, but the untimely death of her loved ones would not be part of it. She brought out a sealed document from her sleeve.

"The details are clearly stated. Nothing in the royal edicts prevents me from transferring everything to you. I'm the widow of a sovereign and control my own destiny."

Geneviève snatched the paper from Nicole's light grasp. Scanning it quickly, the evildoer's eyes began to dance.

"You *were* the widow of a sovereign." Geneviève relaxed into the plush bench seat and stretched out her arms. "My, my, how quickly fortunes can turn."

Instead of Geneviève leaving the coach, Nicole came out. She beamed up at Longdac and sent him on a mad dash to the destination of Grignan's captivity. Then she began walking in the same direction, shoulders square, down the wealthiest streets of Paris, alone. For the last time. She never looked back.

# REVELATIONS AND RESOLUTIONS

# 16

# Le Prix

Garbage fires raged in the dingier sections of the city. Men, women, and children darted around the heat, flying into the squalid streets, scurrying like mice, and chattering nervously that Le Prix had begun.

Athos and Camille sprinted to Notre Dame Cathedral, where people lined up to enter the underground galleries. A festival-like atmosphere wafted through the late afternoon, a cover for the death match. Street performers danced among the spectators. Children knocked sticks about like swords. Along the lines of people, colourful Paris merchants hawked souvenirs, hand-written scorecards, and miniature hand-sewn flags of France.

Athos sent Camille to run up and down the lines to check for Pierre. It might be their one chance to pull him away and dodge peril. As he scouted, Athos jostled through another string of people, several of whom recognized him. Shouts of encouragement filled the air. Tonight, of all nights, his own countrymen knew that Athos and men of his reputation would be milling about for a reason. Athos was a competitor as sure as Anne of Austria was their queen.

Unfamiliar faces swarmed about the streets, and he soon had little room to move between bodies and groups. A zealous set of drinkers locked sights on Athos and surrounded him as if he were their saving grace. Lurching forward through the throng under a stone archway, Athos lost freedom of movement, caught by the undertow of the human current. His admirers swept him down the passageway toward the Gallery of Souls, typically revered as a meditative gateway to the tombs below. Today, the raucous masses filled the echo chamber with the roar of revelry.

A song of Old France—from the days of the Crusades— erupted from a corner and raced like a serpentine fuse across the swath of tightly packed people. Every capable voice rose up. In the tradition of hard-fought battles, the song was a good choice.

*Swing fine swift blades*
*Across thine path*
*For God and country,*
*and our King's wrath.*

Athos joined for one chorus. Dying for a good reason, a risk he was willing to accept, added a prideful third-dimension to his cause.

The throng jockeyed about, pushing and pulling and pressing against the stone walls of the Gallery of Souls. Athos recruited a few of his more enthusiastic new friends to hoist him up to get a better look. Heads and hats and scarves bobbed in the undulating crowd. Not a familiar face among them, a thousand or more strong. Athos guessed Camille to be in the same predicament, though not at the centre of attention.

For what seemed like an hour, the place swelled to over-capacity. Breathing room only. Athos found better footing on the notch of a stone column. His head and shoulders stuck above the human sea. On the lookout, he primed his patience for the next act.

∞∞∞

Jeanne and Pierre congratulated themselves on being ahead of the crowd. As always, her insider information came through. They were among the first to gather in the Gallery of Souls, near a platform raised for the dueling arena. The only drawback—spending the night in the damp gallery, chilled to the bone among the beggars and thieves and rats. He was thankful when warmer bodies started to arrive.

Jeanne contributed her high sweet voice to the rallying songs and cheers. Pierre observed her in her element, among the people she'd grown up with and the familiar ways of peasant life in the city. To the children, she passed out dates from her bag; to the elderly, warm smiles and hugs. Poor but not without vitality, the forgotten people of Paris embraced life as it came. The smarting pain from his fresh wound lessened a bit.

The hodgepodge of sights and sounds created a strange feeling inside Pierre. Life here, in the mass of humanity, was exciting and raw. But he didn't quite fit in. As had many Parisians, he'd known poverty and hard work. Like them, he'd thought his life to be miserable. The lowliest of the low. But in Paris, he saw his previous servitude had not been as awful as it seemed. At Nicole's estate, he had the liberty to run freely between green fields and thick woods. Life in Rochefort had its benefits, an austere yet eloquent simplicity and security. Warm nights, good meals. Too far away now.

He bunched his coat tighter around his chest, and hopped from foot to foot to generate warmth.

"You look a little pewtered," Jeanne said, interrupting her singing.

"Perturbed," he said, hopping faster. "I'm cold and my hand hurts."

She planted herself squarely in his view. "You're the Musketeer's apprentice, and this night will be yours."

She kissed him but failed to pacify. He wrinkled his brow.

"When will this benefactor you've spoken of arrive?" Pierre asked, not masking the irritation in his voice. "How will he even find us in this crowd?"

"Don't worry," Jeanne said at a break in the chorus and handed him a small flask. "He won't have to find us."

A clamour of cowbells began in a far corner of the gallery. The clanging bounced off the stone walls, intensifying in volume. Something important was about to begin.

∞∞∞∞

Nicole stepped into d'Artagnan's apartment two hours after leaving Geneviève's company. Feet aching, she kicked her Italian heels into a corner of the humble quarters. The place was empty. Her heart felt similarly void.

Surprisingly, she arrived before Longdac. She presumed he would have found Grignan and delivered him back to the apartment well before her return. But the streets were in semi-chaos from the oncoming Prix. Athos was surely among them. Where, she had no clue.

On her way upstairs, she had longed for a drink of water but hadn't seen the landlady. She planted herself in a chair at d'Artagnan's table and stared at the grooves worked into the top of the grain. The table had obviously never been a prized possession, just a place to eat a meal or play a game of cards. Next to a candlestick with no candle lay a loose stack of papers. It took Nicole a moment to recognize them. *Sibonne's letters.* Before, they had always been wrapped with a black ribbon. Without it, they simply looked ordinary. Absent importance.

She touched the stack but drew her hand back. Athos had finally given them to Pierre.

She'd contemplated many times after Sibonne's death whether to read them. Yet she always honoured Sibonne's wish that they be read by only one person. Her son. A sharp stab of grief and resignation stung Nicole's throat. Finally, more than eighteen years after her death, this mission had been accomplished. Whether the contents meant anything to the young man was out of her control.

She couldn't visualize Pierre's reaction. Understanding? A sense of finality? Love? Loss? It hinged on the contents of the letters. Nicole always assumed they explained why his mother had orphaned him. Unbound, on the table, inches from Nicole's grasp, the stack of letters lay still. Inside, she wrestled to keep her promise.

# 17

# The Competitors

The Jack of Spades, dressed like a harlequin, sprung to the raised platform. Wearing diamond-patterned red and black, purple baubles, tiny silver bells, and silken ribbons, his gaudy costume covered him from shoes to cap. As the self-appointed master of ceremonies, he gripped a glittering megaphone and boomed to even the farthest spectators in the teeming Gallery of Souls, the catacombs of Notre Dame.

"And now the games, which you all desire, begin!" A roar raged through the throng. Men pumped their fists, and women shook bells on thick ropes. "Bring on your best, bring on your most courageous, bring on your fighters who have no rivals, those men who give France its reputation as the Promised Land for duels. Now is the time of Le Prix du Fer!"

Approving squalls swirled through the catacombs. Pierre toned down his own cheers because of the pain in his hand. Yet the excitement made his blood surge, and he searched Jeanne's face for a sign about what to do next. First-time jitters rattled his nerves.

"When do I go up? How will I know? Who will I say is my benefactor, and what about the money?" He didn't give his string of questions time to breathe.

Jeanne patted his head and grinned. "Watch and learn!" Her light mood amped up his anxiety.

The boisterous harlequin strode from one end of the stage to the other, gesturing to every excited onlooker with his substantial staff, topped by a heavy orb of slag. "And when you enter Le Prix, let there be no doubt, this is the line of mortality," he said, sweeping the wand in front of him as if to draw an invisible mark at the arena's edge. "Once you place a foot here, no one leaves alive but the victor!"

Again, the crowd rewarded the speech with a long raucous roar. The enthusiasm showed off Parisians' love of a voluntary violent spectacle.

The emcee waved down the cheers. "But first," he shouted into the megaphone, "the rules!"

The rumours proved true, according to the harlequin's litany of guidelines. Dueling would occur in rounds, depending on the number of players, and each was a man-to-man swordfight to the death. No other weapons could be used. If a sword broke, it would require the weaponless man to fight for control of his competitor's sword. Survivors advanced to the next round, no matter their injuries from the previous. Once a duel started, nothing could end it except the death of an opponent. Not cries for mercy, white flags, or unconsciousness. The only way to escape death involved forfeiting between rounds. It also meant a shame much greater than the weight of Earth on Atlas.

"To this day," the colourful emcee forewarned, a crooked smile forming, "none has forfeited."

The entrance fees bestowed a small fortune on the winner. "That is, if none of you skimmed the cream!" The harlequin snickered, motioning to the referees, several sturdy men standing and smirking at the back of the raised platform.

"Glory is assured the winner, for the man who takes Le Prix wins the hearts of his beloved countrymen, and no finer shrine could be built than from this astute reputation."

Pierre's desire for redemption leaped. If he prevailed, his prior reputation as the insolent servant who killed an aristocrat would vanish in one night. He would have jumped on the stage that moment had Jeanne not placed on him a wet open-mouthed kiss.

"All the winners so far bought large estates in the country," she said with a wistful look in her eyes. "They never fought again."

Fame. Fortune. An estate of his own.

Pierre grew bolder in the knowledge of the ultimate prize. Respect.

∞∞∞∞

Athos rubbed his shoulder. The old injury troubled him. He had Pierre to thank for surviving his last swordfight, one fraught with so many regrets that Athos didn't care to keep score. If only he had tried harder to stop Pierre from making a scene at Le Louvre … If only he had been more vigilant to save the young man from his ambition … If only Nicole had stayed hidden away from her husband … Then maybe he wouldn't be here, all but reliving a complicated past.

The crowd wanted a show. Athos wanted Pierre. It was too late to find him and stop him from entering.

"Now's the time," the harlequin announced, "to enter the arena!"

Athos decided to wait it out before approaching the stage.

A commotion arose in a far corner of the crowd.

"Here, here!" The harlequin stomped and swung his staff in the direction of the ruckus. "We have our first taker!"

Athos shook his head at the unexpected candidate.

"My name is Remi Tremon," the man bellowed.

A few cheers emerged from the small faction that had served him up. Dressed in hunting attire, he immediately took center stage.

"I fight for the gypsies south of Paris, whose reputation as good and true citizens of France is mine to defend."

A few hisses were drowned out by lukewarm applause. The irony, Athos thought, was that Remi Tremon wasn't even a gypsy, just a fugitive granted acceptance among the nomads. Athos scanned the crowd. If Pierre were looking on and knew his own story, this moment brought him face-to-face for the first time with his father.

∞∞∞∞

Pierre blinked in quick succession. *It couldn't be. How could it be?* But the chances of there being another Remi Tremon in France were next to impossible.

"That man," he whispered in a slight stupor to Jeanne, "that man has my last name."

A bitter taste coated his mouth. The story of his father often did. The man—*this man not twenty feet away*—had left him in servitude with the Comte. Bitterness stirred his ire.

Jeanne took a second glance at Pierre. "Do you know him?"

"No," he said flatly, not a lie. "Never met him in my life."

She shrugged and turned back to Remi, now grandstanding to rile the crowd, as was the obvious tradition. Without prompting, Jeanne explained to Pierre that each swordsman boasted to earn the favour of those who wagered on each match. It was the second most entertaining aspect of Le Prix, the high-pitched betting and shifting allegiances among the spectators. If one group, such as the gypsies, could generate enough excitement for their man, they could also win a wager large enough for a band of them to live off of for an entire year, regardless of their prospects. They often bet against their own men to win.

"He looks beatable," Pierre said, setting his jaw. And, if anyone had a reason to beat him, he did.

"Don't underestimate the gypsies," Jeanne said, nodding toward the Tremon on stage. "They are wily and skilled, though not many of them want much attention."

Pierre wondered if Remi would know who he was when it was his turn to enter. Would it matter? His father had given him up long ago, and in every way, Pierre was a stranger to him. Remi might be vulnerable to manipulation, guilted into showing Pierre mercy. Yet another reason he was beatable.

Pierre took stock. Same build. Same squareness around the eyes. Same upper-body strength. They might pass for kin, but the stakes were what mattered, and in Pierre's estimation, he saw a weaker opponent.

Before Remi ended his introduction, he issued a parting threat, sword held high: "I'm merciless and possess the skill of a thousand duels! When I strike, death strikes."

The last words drew respectable accolades from the crowd as Pierre plotted how his speech would smash the gypsy's to rubble.

But Jeanne held him back again. Except not with a kiss. Her grip dug into his forearm.

"Wait until more opponents come forward," she said in a lower voice. "You'll gain an advantage."

"How? It won't change anything. We'll end up hating each other just the same." Pierre squirmed under her grip.

"Just wait!"

Before they had finished the short argument, two new men had joined the harlequin and Remi. Guards of the Cardinal—

Biscarat and Jussac. The crowd nearly caught fire. In fact, several hats landed on stage ablaze. Pierre couldn't tell if it was in support or derision. The audience's fervor drummed into his temples and delayed the guards' speeches. He wished he could garner a similar enthusiasm, even if from hatred.

The two soldiers grinned and responded by standing with locked fists above their heads, boastful that victory would be theirs. Pierre punched the air hotly in frustration, though no one around him knew the wiser. The exception being Jeanne.

"Your turn will come. Remember, you're the Musketeer's apprentice."

Pierre's face burned hotter than the sweaty stew surrounding him. If he based the size of the crowd on the attendance at mass in Rochefort—then doubled it, quadrupled it, thrice-over—this group most likely exceeded one thousand. He'd never stood among so many.

Biscarat finally fired off a short treatise about entering for the glory of the Church. He vowed God would win this year's Prix.

"I bet my life on it!"

Jussac immediately took that bet. "But," he said, "it may pit guard against guard." With that, the crowd both jeered and boomed with excitement. A few buxom young admirers near the front of the stage peeled off several dramatic squeals. Pierre hoped he, too, could muster a few of the damsels' tears.

"Surely, they'd forfeit if it came to that," Pierre said almost under his breath.

"Not likely," Jeanne said shaking her head. "Which guard wants to go down in history as the first man to ever forfeit Le Prix? A mouse would earn more respect."

Pierre pushed forward a few steps, stunned by the next entrant, a man who plagued his past and future.

Vachon.

"I can tell you know this one," Jeanne said close to his ear.

He swatted at her like a buzzing gnat.

She smiled. "Because you suddenly got bloodluck in your eyes!"

"Bloodlust—*lust*," he emphasized, annoying a few nearby spectators. He could feel his darker instincts rising, too, same as the day he killed the Comte. Pierre wanted this opponent more than any man in France.

"This is turning out better than I'd hoped," Jeanne said, in a quiet aside to herself. But Pierre overhead her and also felt the same.

"I'm glad you made me wait," he admitted.

"I could be the next Joan of Art."

"Arc," he murmured, not quite understanding the connection.

∞∞∞

Athos caught himself holding his breath, as if waiting for a cannonball to blast. If anything were to bring Pierre out of hiding, Vachon sealed it.

Hardly ten seconds had passed before Pierre commandeered the platform, sword drawn, upstaging Vachon. Vachon took all of two blinks to recognize the disheveled Pierre, whose short-cropped hair stood on end. Even since Athos's last contact, Pierre had lost weight and had a newly bandaged hand. His natural boldness, however, had multiplied.

A sea change occurred in the crowd, from controlled mayhem to cackling hysteria. Many below Athos jostled for better position, almost ruining his view. He repositioned himself on the post to watch the outcome unfold.

"Whoa-ho-ho!" The harlequin foisted his body between the two swordsmen. "Men of Le Prix! Remember your honour!"

The rules of the underground contest were still the rules. Ironically, spontaneous duels were forbidden. In scarlet-gloved hands, the harlequin firmly pushed the tips of the two men's blades down below his navel. "My dear fellows," he said, not giving an inch, "if you will kindly yield."

A half dozen referees surrounded the overzealous contestants, each wielding a weapon of choice. A knife, a club, a chain, a whip, and in a few cases, more than one. Even a few rogues in the crowd waved sticks.

The harlequin cleared his throat as the two rivals slowly came to their senses and lowered their weapons. "Now," he continued, "we have yet to hear from our first gallant sire. You, upstart, must step aside!" With this, the emcee brushed the dingy lapels of Pierre's coat, a more-than-subtle sign of his lowliness. Athos swallowed back a lump of pride, a mere pebble compared to the boulder that Pierre was probably choking down.

Vachon's chest grew a good two inches as Pierre reluctantly stood down.

Vachon returned his sword to its scabbard and bowed to the audience, who lauded him with happy cheers. Women threw kisses, and a few toddlers were propped on shoulders.

"My fellow Parisians," he began, "my name is Vachon, one of this city's sons. My home is Paris, where my family overcame great challenges so that I could become a man of the sword. For this, I earned praise from French noblemen near and far, as the protector of land, property, and people, as a foot soldier. I accepted every assignment with great pride. I relished a job well done.

"However, this came at an awful cost. My last assignment wrought a terrible outcome—the death of my equally honourable brother, Henri, no finer a brother or Frenchman. While executing his orders, this interloper," he pointed to Pierre, "viciously killed him without cause. He cowardly back-stabbed my brother for nothing more than a horse. Henri never knew he was at risk, could not defend himself in a duel, and died alone with no opportunity to counter the unprovoked attack."

Pierre puckered in contempt and crossed his hands over his chest, feet planted firmly apart. Athos caught, for the first time, a glimmer of patience in Pierre. He was biding his time to tell the real story.

"Now, I stand before you, a lesser man, a brotherless man, seeking to honour Henri with a victory for all of Paris!"

As expected, the story stoked the crowd's enthusiasm. Their whoops and whistles surpassed those for the previous men and caused deep wrinkles between Pierre's brows.

"You," Vachon shouted, "took a good man's life. You give me reason to fight—to avenge him!" Yet another wave of cheers boomed from the audience. Pierre stood stock still, staring down his challenger. Spotty chants of *Va-chon Va-chon Va-chon* began, but the harlequin stepped in to move the ceremonies along.

"We'll now hear from the man of the ire," he chuckled, and bent to whisper in Pierre's ear, who returned to the brief exchange, "a man who wishes to be known as The Musketeer's Apprentice."

The harlequin uncharacteristically grabbed Pierre by the bandaged hand and raised it above their heads. Athos noticed no flinch, probably because the greater pain in Pierre had nothing to do with his body. The crowd gave a tepid round of applause likely due to Pierre's appearance. Missing a finger, scant from starvation, and bedeviled by a new injury made him the picture of scourge.

As the harlequin backed away, Pierre sternly stared down the crowd from one end of the cave-like hall to the other. Whispers and a few heckles swirled through the mass.

He responded with a lengthy silence. The only sounds that withstood were a few babies crying in the back. The unnerving slow buildup could have kept a King's army at bay.

"There are among you," he started after a deep breath, "the most humble of France." He made eye contact with several peasants whose hunger clung to their baggy skin. "I am one of you."

A few nodded back.

"We're the forgotten. The tread-upon. The misunderstood. We toil in the fields and laundries and ironworks and stables, wrapping the rich in golden cloth and filling their days with leisure. We survive, unseen and discarded," he said, stretching a hand to several near the front. "You know that no matter what we do or who we serve, we'll never be like them. Not in a hundred years, not in a thousand years, not even as a winner of Le Prix."

Small clusters in the crowd nodded with him and amongst themselves. Murmurs came from many sides. "I know this because that's all I've ever known. I've served under the wealthiest of France and taken solace in small comforts—a warm fire, a savoury broth, a clean bed—things they take for granted. Yet, they think these comforts are grand when they give them. We know better. Benevolence in a cage never tastes like liberty."

Athos's heart tumbled. Pierre wasn't giving Nicole credit for the small freedoms she'd granted him, far more liberally than most nobles. Peasantry was still peasantry. Bondage, still bondage.

"You may know me as the man who killed the Comte de Rochefort. For months, I've rotted in the Bastille and believed it to be my doom. But fate brings me here, and despite what you've heard," he said, glancing at Vachon, "the deaths by my sword are justifiable. Vachon and his brother Henri knew me as a deliverer of justice."

Agreement emerged from the men. "I killed his brother because of his brutal behaviour toward a woman he laid no claim to. He deserved to die and suffer the repercussions. Privilege does grant men immunity. We, my fellow French countrymen, pose a threat to the nobility. When we think and act for ourselves and demand opportunity and fairness, we can be unstoppable."

Whoops and faint chants of "*Solidarité*" filled the gallery. "Like you," Pierre interrupted, "my oppression began as a child by the hands of men whom Vachon and his brother choose to serve. He kissed their boots and any part of them stuck in his face." Laughter broke out. "Now, as a man, my oppression ends once and for all. In this arena! By might and by will! I reclaim legitimacy with this sword!"

Holding his sword high above his head, no other words were necessary. Approval swept from one end of the crowd to the other. The lusty echoes whipped around the caverns. Pierre had aroused a collective disharmony. Every hopeless soul found a spark in him. He'd spoken the lament of the downtrodden. For the first time since Athos could recall, a generation seemed to have found a lightning rod.

Athos wanted to share the *espirit de corps*, but his past rendered him a sympathetic outsider. His lineage set him apart. Despite the Musketeer status he faithfully honoured, his background as a nobleman—a life he scarcely claimed any more—linked him to privilege.

And, he was next.

# 18

# Paris Stands Still

The last letter slipped from Nicole's hand and floated to the floorboards. It came to rest near the other letters. The blood rushed in her ears, and her throat constricted.

"How could this be? What have I done?" Had she spoken aloud?

The words in her sister's letters, strewn across the floor, seemed foreign, beyond translation. Her hand passed over the disordered stack. The neat creases and folds had fooled her into a state of hope. Once, their promise had saved her from many regrets. She realized now that regrets haunted her and her sister's path at every turn.

Had Pierre read them? How could he not have? What might become of him? Her temples throbbed. She had to reach him, unsure exactly what to say.

∞∞∞

Athos needed no introduction. As soon as he climbed the stage and faced the mass of people, his commanding presence held every gaze in the gallery. A thick air of national pride imbued the crowd, as evidenced in the squaring of men's shoulders and beaming of women's faces. His people's veneration bonded the group.

The harlequin's bells jangled, a friendly reminder that the rules still applied, even to a man of the King. To achieve his goal, Athos needed every sympathy. He nodded toward the emcee.

"It's my sincerest honour, Monsieur Athos. We salute you and grant you the stage." The harlequin bowed, pausing several seconds longer than necessary. "May I present the legendary and revered Musketeer, Athos! Most esteemed protector of our King!"

The room inhaled, and heads bowed. Athos bowed in return.

"Thank you, my countrymen and women. You must wonder why a servant of the King, such as myself, would cast his lot in this fatal contest. I'm humbled by your enthusiasm for each competitor braving imminent death." Athos sent a quick glance to the row of competitors. The group, including Pierre, stared cautiously at him, masking their hatred. "Each of us has our own reasons for being here."

A few grumbles drifted from the men. Athos took no offense. He drank the crowd in, for he was truly amazed. Here, the people had found a way to bond beyond their everyday indignations. The sheer energy they needed to survive left them so few outlets of release that Le Prix—a death sport—became an ironic rescue from their spiritual poverty.

"My reasons for being here differ from my competitors," he resumed. "The prospect of glory and wealth do not bring me before you. There are those of us, despite our assumed privilege, who operate for greater good, often when greater good seems elusive." Many heads bobbed, and a few of the miniature flags of France waved in approval. "Yet, you give me hope! You've shown me today that the blood still races in your veins. The ordinary does not interest you, and on this stage, peril and possibility collide. You yearn for the extraordinary. In this moment, you rise above despair!"

The racket from the men, women, and children thundered beneath Athos's feet. But he raised his hands and shook his head. "No, no, no," he waved them down and waited. "Hear me out! My awe has an underbelly."

A few groups started chanting his name, but he kept shaking his head. "Death is not glory!" He shouted, cutting the chanting in half. "These men lay down their lives, for the slight chance of what? False victory? Death without an honourable cause? The spoils from spilled blood? I present myself as one who wants to live!" He pulled the Musketeer tabard over his head and flung it to the ground. "I want to live! And, I will compete for my life! For my precious life … and also another's."

The row of competitors began eying each other. Except for one. "That person knows who he is," Athos went on, "and he knows why I'm here." A few moments passed.

"If it comes down to you and me," Pierre said, just loud enough for only the group onstage to hear, "I won't hesitate to kill you."

Athos frowned at his troubled young friend. He lamented how he'd changed. Aged. Hardened. Become dispirited and also wiser. "I would expect nothing less."

Pierre huffed, and his upper lip twitched.

"What of your injuries?" Athos asked, as if no one else were there.

"Don't underestimate me," was the rebuke. "You won't stand in my way."

Athos returned his focus to the nattering audience, back to reality, but he reached out to Pierre, and in a calm voice, announced: "Pierre Tremon brings me to your Prix. I'm here to save his life."

∞∞∞∞

No sooner were the words spoken than the emcee shouted: "We have our competitors!" The entry period was over. The slate of swordsmen stood cocksure. Gleefully, the harlequin leaped and danced in black-and-red streaks in front of the men.

Remi, the gypsy pursuing fortune.

Biscarat, the Cardinal's premier guard.

Jussac, his equally accomplished strongman.

Vachon, the brother seeking revenge.

Pierre, the Musketeer's Apprentice.

And, Athos, the only man without an ambition for glory.

The harlequin took an encore to please the masses. Then, he formed the all-important pre-fight huddle. He gathered the band of referees and the six swordsmen, shoulder to shoulder. Athos and Pierre glared at each other from opposing sides.

"Let's hold our daggers for the actual fight," the harlequin directed the two. "Right now, we have the matter of the entry fees."

Pierre's pulse quickened. He looked over his shoulder into the crowd, desperate for a glimpse of his lifeline, Jeanne. He spotted her bright red hair bobbing three layers deep in the crowd.

In order of entry, each man produced the name of a benefactor and a pouch of pistoles. Pierre came second to last.

"And you?" the harlequin quizzed.

"My benefactor is … is …" Pierre stammered, trying not to make eye contact with any of the others, "… is … in the crowd."

The harlequin glanced into the gallery. "Well, who is it, and where's your entry fee?"

Pierre stepped back from the circle and waved to Jeanne. She waved vigorously back and convinced the spectators around her to hand her over to the stage. She flopped on the edge, and Pierre tugged her up by the waist. She brushed herself off and walked confidently into the circle of men.

"Well, well, well," said the harlequin, a slight twinkle in his eye. "If it isn't the infamous damsel Jeanne." He eyed her suspiciously as several referees shuffled their feet impatiently behind him. Pierre remembered she would have been a familiar face from the gambling house.

"My darling, you can't tell me that *you* are the benefactor of this tenacious boy." The harlequin tsked-tsked and shook his head.

"Of course not! He has much higher friends."

"Well then, whom?" The harlequin shook his staff and bells in her face.

"Cardinal Richelieu himself."

"What?!" Pierre blurted.

"Oh, this is getting good," the harlequin nodded, going from her expression to his.

"I'm sorry, Pierre, but anyone who escapes the Bastille is also a wanted man." She batted her eyes and forced an innocent smile. "I told the Cardinal that for a nice sum I could provide information about your whereabouts. So, in one way, he's your benefactor." She plopped a bag of coins into the harlequin's outstretched hand.

"If the Cardinal knew his whereabouts, the entire Prix would be closed down by now," Jussac fired off skeptically. The harlequin was too busy with his nose stuck in the coin bag.

"I may have fibbed a little about the timing of the match," she demurred, squinting between her thumb and forefinger.

"A little!?" Pierre shouted.

The harlequin's amusement vanished. "How much time do we have?"

"An hour before dawn."

Several sighed in relief.

"Why use the money on him?" said Jussac. "Why not give him up and go on your way?"

She nodded. "Yes, that would have been the safest bet, wouldn't it?"

The harlequin's smile returned incrementally. "Ah, Jeanne, your true colors shine so brightly. She's holding the Cardinal off, aren't you, my dear, so she can win more by betting on one of these fine men. You probably think you know who'll win."

She air-kissed the harlequin.

Pierre threw up his arms and stalked to the edge of the stage, speechless.

She followed him, grabbed him by the upper arm, and pecked his cheek. "Don't be sore, my love. I'm betting on you."

∞∞∞

Everything seemed out of the ordinary and nothing did. Athos declared his benefactor, the Comtesse de Rochefort, which surprised no one though Vachon ground his teeth. Athos kept to himself the detail that Nicole was in Paris. Bickering then ensued among the men because of complications introduced by Jeanne, who was banished from the stage. Her tipoff to the Cardinal gave everyone a bone to pick.

"What if we're raided before the final round?" Biscarat demanded of no one in particular.

"We could all end up in the Bastille! I can't fight the Cardinal's men alone if I've killed most of you," Remi boasted, but only slightly.

"The two of you are already working for the Cardinal!" Vachon leveled at Biscarat and Jussac. "How do we know you aren't already in on his plans? Either way, you'll avoid persecution."

The group hotly discussed moving the duel to another location, but the idea was quickly dismissed. The sheer size of the crowd ruled it out. No less, the spectators were starting to catcall and demand the first match.

Using his staff like a gavel, the harlequin pounded the floor to halt the debate. "Enough! Enough! We're wasting time! Le Prix must start!"

Athos noticed Pierre sizing everyone up. They'd arrived at the point of no return, the brink of the game itself. Only one would live to see daybreak, unless Athos and Pierre were the last two in the arena and the forfeit card was played. One complication mired his plan: if Pierre were killed first. Athos couldn't imagine an easy way to victory.

Each man drew straws. Round one struck at the heart of the drama.

*Remi versus Pierre.*

The first formal introduction of father and son.

Remi tried an attack, but Pierre counter-parried and swiped the back of Remi's dominant hand. The long cut quickly grew bloody, and Remi grabbed it and clenched his jaw. His sword stayed firmly in hand.

"My mother is Sibonne, the youngest daughter of the Comte de Rochefort." Pierre nodded as Remi's expression grew more unsettled. "She had a son. *Your son.* I am your son."

Remi shook his head. He mouthed the word *no*, but his stare conveyed something else. Pierre's waist throbbed, and he involuntarily grabbed the wound. It wasn't that he felt much pain; he wanted to feel real pain, something other than the lifelong anguish because his father had chosen to give him away.

Remi winced and squeezed his hand harder. Pierre should have seized the chance to kill him then, but he wanted more than his swift end. How could a father give up his son—*his only son*—to be doomed to servitude?

"Father!" a man's voice bellowed from the crowd.

Before Pierre could see him, a second distraction erupted in another section of the gallery. Cries for "*Water, water!*" rose above a section of kneeling spectators. Pierre turned back to the fight, growing impatient.

"Why did you give me up?! I'm your son!" His anger spilled in a flood.

"You're not my son," Remi said, looking toward the crowd.

"Even in the face of defeat, you lie!"

"I'm not your father!" Remi pointed with his chin. "There, that man there, he's my son."

By then, a man of Pierre's age and height had pulled himself onto the stage. His clean-cut looks, wide-eyed expression, and dusty red hair reminded him of Nicole.

The young man hesitated, and the three held an awkward space.

Remi frowned. "You shouldn't have come up here."

A connection linked the two. A blink. A nod. They spoke their own body language. Pierre's jealousy curled like smoke.

The harlequin jumped into the centre of the trio. "This won't do!" He slammed his staff down and gestured to a burly referee, who immediately confronted the son.

The young man protested and resisted a shoulder-hold. "I can be my father's second. The rules allow it. You cannot deny a second!"

"I won't have it!" Remi shouted. He took his sword by his uninjured hand. It looked out of place, a fatal mistake waiting to happen. Pierre wanted to explode, more so because he wanted the truth rather than Remi Tremon's death. He stomped toward the harlequin.

"I refuse to fight a second! And you there—" Pierre pointed to the younger man. At the same time, the interloper broke away from the referee with his sword drawn. Pierre blocked several attacks but refused to be baited into a duel. A fight with a second wasn't the one Pierre had come for.

While in mid-parry, Pierre shouted to Remi. "Old gypsy! Control him or I'll kill him!"

Remi dove into the fight, both taming the son's attacks while also delivering a few of his own. The harlequin dodged the shuffling men, pulled the referee away, and let the threesome have at it.

Pierre raged into an offense. In full-body strikes, he landed blows to both men's swords in one swoop. Instinctively, he disarmed the injured Remi, claiming his sword in a few adroit moves. One punctured his shoulder. Unarmed and wounded again, Remi froze and dismay fell over him.

Pierre lunged at the son, a mirror version of himself when he had first met Athos. Memories of his first lessons with the Musketeer raced forward. His rambunctiousness. His over-confidence. His vulnerability. Dreams of grandeur. It almost seemed a shame to kill his challenger's potential.

But kill, he must. If for no other reason than to kill. And, kill, Pierre did.

# A Son Revealed

Sword held high, Pierre towered over the stage, the son dead by a clean mid-body strike. Accolades were few and short. A shrill cry turned heads toward a commotion in the gallery.

Just as suddenly, Remi tackled Pierre to the floor. Blood from the gypsy's injuries covered Pierre and splattered the stage. Swords spun across the platform. Remi headlocked Pierre and beat his face again and again on the floor. Pierre gasped for air. After countless blows, there was no distinguishing whose blood was whose.

Athos and three referees pounced on Remi and struggled to wrestle him off the nearly unconscious Pierre. Manhandling him, they immobilized Remi, who gnashed his teeth and spewed epithets while trying to kick and punch his way free; the men held him somehow.

Ear-piercing shrieks from a woman in the crowd grew louder, longer, and closer; their mournfulness even paused Remi's struggle.

Pierre, sight failing, heard the shrieks clearly. He thought it was a banshee. He hoped it was a specter. Her cries defined the meaning of agony.

Athos lunged into the crowd toward the sound.

Before Pierre could whisper the name *Nicole*, he passed out.

∞∞∞

Athos snaked between spectators until he found her. She was on the verge of collapse. Tears streaked her blotchy face, and pink splotches covered her flushed neck. He caught Nicole, unprepared for the heaviness of her spirit.

"My God, why are you here?!" There was nowhere to go, and bystanders crowded them. "Get back," he yelled, waving them off. He lifted her into his arms, and she sobbed into his chest.

"Take me to him."

Athos slowly picked a path through the tight bodies and called to Biscarat and Jussac to lift her onstage. As soon as Athos leapt up, he took her into his arms.

Regaining her breath, she turned timidly to the carnage. Pierre lay as still as a corpse, and next to him, the dead young man. Remi wrestled again to be free, and the men released him. He fell on his son's body and heaved in rough sobs, wailing: *No! This cannot be. Not my son. No! Anything but this.*

Nicole took a step, but Athos held her fast. Every day since Nicole had accepted his love, he had thanked God. Now perfection fell prey to reality. He didn't understand why she'd come, even less so after she folded into him again, crying. He urged, "There's nothing to be gained here."

Nicole looked toward Pierre and nodded to move closer. "Bring water," Athos shouted, knowing it probably wouldn't help.

Nicole knelt by Pierre as a bucket was placed nearby, and Athos rung a rag. She tried brushing a wisp of hair from his eyes; the sticky blood on his face kept it down.

"Let me," Athos said and began dabbing. He listened for breathing and nodded affirmatively.

"He's so damaged," she began before a wave of calm washed over her.

"You shouldn't be here," Athos pleaded. "This is only cruelty."

His gentle rebuke made no inroads. She kept her gaze on Pierre.

"What aren't you telling me?" Athos gently caught her hand before she touched Pierre again.

"I read her letters."

Athos let her hand go. "You finally gave in."

"They provided a detail that changes everything."

He couldn't fathom. He searched her eyes for an answer.

She closed them. "Pierre's not hers."

Athos tightened his grip on the bloody rag. "Are you certain?"

"Yes. Absolutely."

"Does he know?"

"If he read the letters, he would know."

"Then ..." Athos turned toward Remi and the young man who lay dead.

Nicole's gaze followed. "Is he dead?"

Athos stared intensely at the carnage. "I don't know."

She buckled over and wept into Pierre's collar.

The scrape of a blade slipping from its scabbard cut the unfolding drama. Vachon stood over them with a contemptuous grin. "A fine match you make. Always in the middle of a mess."

"Let it go, Vachon, you'll get your chance later," Athos said but didn't bother to raise his voice or stand.

"Yes, but more likely if I challenge you to a duel right now."

Athos rose and planted his heels. "Your ego never sits out."

Before Athos could draw his sword, the harlequin popped in with a jangle. "Problem, gentlemen?"

"I challenge Athos to a duel."

"During Le Prix?" The harlequin scratched beneath his gaudy hat and screwed one eyebrow. "Very unorthodox—but not outside the realm of possibility."

"No!" Nicole interjected, still kneeling at Pierre. "I won't allow it."

"I'm sorry to inform you, Madame ... Comtesse Rochefort, isn't it?" The harlequin shook his head. "Your influence has no purchase here."

"I'm no longer a Comtesse."

"Come again?" the harlequin leaned in sideways.

"I'm not the Comtesse de Rochefort."

The harlequin cackled and spun twice around. "And I am the King of Spain!"

Athos knelt to her. "What are you saying?"

She approached Vachon and squared her shoulders. "I've made a pact with your benefactor that you are no longer allowed to harm me or anyone in my circle of influence. If this agreement is broken, she loses the Comte's estate and forfeits her newly acquired fortune and title."

Vachon leaned on his sword and rubbed a temple. "You're telling me that you've given up your wealth *and* title—everything—to save this Musketeer and that scoundrel?" he asked and pointed his sword at Pierre.

She nodded. "Them and everyone I love."

Sighing heavily, Vachon shook his head and sheathed the sword. "That's the most outlandish trade I've ever heard, and one so preposterous, it should be false, but coming from you ..."

She bristled a little at his envious gaze. She had what every man wanted, a devotion so intense that she would give up everything for her lover.

Athos came to her rescue, pulling her into him and uttering his disbelief. She kissed him to stop his rambling and offered her rationale, only between them. "No riches could ever replace you."

The harlequin capitalized on the news. In a few boastful outbursts about the transcendence of love, the entire audience knew the details of the Comtesse's arrangement and began celebrating with whoops and congratulatory hollers from every corner of the gallery.

"Who doesn't love True Love! Although, this does change the nature of our Prix," the harlequin grumbled into his megaphone, "as does the defeat of not one, not two, but three challengers!" To whom he swiveled around and swept his arms. One dead, one unconscious, and one slightly wounded but standing. "This game has gotten a little more complicated."

"In more ways than one," said Jussac, and he grabbed both of the harlequin's wrists and bound him with a thin strap.

"You're next," Biscarat declared and headed straight for Athos, who'd seen it coming. While scrambling in the crowd for Nicole, he'd recognized several faces, all of them Cardinal's guards.

"Get out of here," Athos blurted and turned Nicole to the back of the stage and pointed to a passageway below. At the edge, she paused.

More guards advanced the stage, and both Athos and Vachon jumped into defense mode. Amid the mayhem, Nicole found a necessary vein of courage and headed toward Remi, who seemed oblivious to the sudden discord. She gathered his shaky hands and fought back her own trembling. "Monsieur, my utmost sympathy."

Remi raised his bloodshot eyes.

"I'm so very, very sorry." Inadequate, she knew. "I don't know if you know me. I'm Sibonne's sister."

His mouth opened, but words never formed.

"It's all right," she squeezed his hands. "I've never forgotten her."

They both looked at Remi's dead son. And, maybe, her nephew. She needed to know, and there was only one way to find out.

"My sister left letters for her son. Her letters say he had a distinct birthmark at the base of his scalp near his left ear. It was the shape of a large teardrop. Does any of this sound right to you?"

But Nicole might as well have been talking to a stone turret. Remi just stared bleary-eyed at the dead young man.

She knelt, placed a hand on the slain man's shoulder, moved his head gently to one side, and ran her fingers through his red hair. It parted enough to finally put the mystery to rest.

# Mayhem and Madness

Behind Nicole, the sword fight raged on. Taking one inhale and exhale, she moved swiftly and deliberately. She had to escape, but she wished one last moment with Pierre.

Protectively, Athos fought in front of Pierre's body. Camille had finally arrived onstage to fight at his side. Vachon flanked them, and together the three were holding back six guards. Many of the women and children in the audience had fled, but several intrepid hotheads below were using sticks and raw vegetables to pummel the Cardinal's men.

"Leave! Now!" Athos shouted to Nicole.

"I love you!" she shouted back and bent down to Pierre's ear.

"Pierre, can you hear me?" She thought she saw an eyelid flutter. "Pierre, I love you. I need you to go to safety. You must try. I want you to know there's more to your story. You'll always be my family but not by blood. You have a chance for true freedom."

Behind her, Jeanne materialized, a few wiry hairs astray, but none the worse for the chaos. "Here," she said and threw down a blanket. "We'll drag him out!"

The two clumsily rolled his body atop the blanket and yanked it to the back of the stage. Athos, fighting Biscarat one-on-one, pleaded for the women to leave him behind.

"You're such an opportunist," Biscarat taunted at a pause in the fight. "First you seduce the Comte's wife, and now you tell her to abandon her family. Musketeer honour at its best."

"I should be fighting him!" Athos flicked his head toward Vachon, adding sarcastically, "Now you've gone and ruined everything."

But exhaustion bore down. Athos felt his strength slipping away. His weak shoulder was incapable of a drawn-out fight, so he took a chance and jumped down into the maniacal crowd. Biscarat jumped after him.

As Athos had hoped, the crowd rallied behind him and heaped their fury onto the Cardinal's man. Rather than Biscarat, The Enforcer, he was Biscarat, The Subdued. Like a swarm of locust, several overzealous spectators pounded him to the floor, leaving Athos an opening to escape. For the first time in recent memory, rather than feel disdain, Athos appreciated the rabid adoration of his people.

# 22

# Full Circle

Both Jeanne and Nicole hesitated at the opening of the dim and narrow catacombs below the stage. They had no knowledge, compass, or map to guide them. With little choice, they forged into the gray-black and dragged Pierre as best they could. Afraid of bats, Nicole ducked at flutters inside the stone tunnel, a relic from the Crusades. Back then, escape routes meant life or death.

Athos arrived hastily and scooped Pierre into his arms. Camille showed up not far behind, and the two took the lead.

"Follow closely," Athos said, darting forward. "And don't look back."

Athos pushed on through a byzantine series of turns and switchbacks. Several felt illogical. No pattern or reason ruled the route.

"How do you know the way?" Nicole asked. The damp air coated her throat.

"Years of living in peril," he said with an effortless wink.

Echoes of their movement in the tunnel turned into a ghostly cacophony from all sides. Were they being followed? Tracked by the guard? Sought in revenge by a revived Remi? If the way was far, Nicole worried her growing fatigue would jeopardize the escape. The baby depleted her of needed energy after an already emotional night. And, she saw Athos's strength waning with each step carrying Pierre through the stone maze.

Camille must have noticed, too, and gathered Pierre from Athos, excusing it as his turn. Nicole shared a knowing glance. They needed to find a safe haven soon.

After what seemed like an hour, a funnel of brighter light appeared ahead. Athos halted and told them to wait and vanished toward it. Their labored breathing filled the emptiness. Nicole leaned into the stone wall and murmured a short prayer.

Pierre's eyes fluttered open, not quite the answer she had expected.

Prone at Camille's feet, Pierre felt clammy to her touch. Large bruises, scraps, scabs, and welts covered his face from Remi's beating. He blinked rapidly, but light didn't seem to get in.

She motioned to Jeanne. "The blanket."

This loosened his tongue. "It can't be," he blurted. Fear, or something akin to it, crossed his face. "No!" And the scream ricocheted down the passageway like a stray bullet.

"No, what?" Nicole said quietly, hoping to calm him.

"I won't go back! Never!" He tried lifting up, but his neck couldn't support his head.

Nicole looked at everyone, confused.

"The Bastille," Jeanne interrupted. "It's a lot like this place. Even if he can't see it, it smells the same."

Loamy. Dank. Full of rot and decay and hopelessness.

Nicole nodded. Jeanne's larger part in Pierre's life sank in.

"Help me! Help me! Don't leave me here!" Pierre covered his ears.

"We're with you," Nicole said. She rubbed his shoulders and searched for better words.

"He's delusional," Camille told her and turned toward the direction Athos had gone. "It might take him a while to come out of it."

Nicole shushed and reassured Pierre, but he whimpered on. He pleaded as if she were a stranger.

"Can you help?" she asked Jeanne.

Jeanne took a knee and patted Pierre on the head and chest. "There, there, my love. We'll be out of here as soon as your Musketeer friend finds us a ride."

Pierre's eyes widened a little, either because of Jeanne's voice or the mention of the Musketeer. Slowly, the young woman came into Pierre's focus. Jeanne, though handsome, suffered from calloused hands, hollow cheeks, hard living. But her spirit out-shined it. It wasn't hard to understand her appeal to Pierre though Nicole hoped that the nature of their liaison had been purely platonic.

"That's my Pierre," Jeanne said and landed a sloppy kiss on his busted lips.

So much for chastity.

As soon as Jeanne raised up, his expression turned cold. "You … you double-crossed me!"

He grabbed her by the hair and began scolding her. Between Jeanne's yelps, Camille intervened to keep Pierre steadfastly down. Pierre succeeded in snatching a few strands of Jeanne's hair.

"Ho, you there!" A voice traveled down the stoneway, and Camille peered back at the light.

A scuffle took place out of their view. Camille took out his sword and headed for the noise.

"What about us?" Nicole called.

"Stay here," he said, waving her back. "You'll know what to do."

Of this, she was perfectly uncertain.

It took less than a minute for her to follow him out.

∞∞∞

"Go back, Nicole!"

Athos gagged the words out from a chokehold. Remi stood behind him. At a deserted street-level marketplace, trouble had come to call. Empty tables and benches encircled the four: Nicole, Camille, and Athos, subdued by the vengeful gypsy.

"Gypsies have an uncanny ability to track people," Camille whispered to Nicole.

"Send Pierre up!" Remi shouted from his corner of the market.

"He can't walk," Nicole finally called back. "You beat him too terribly."

"If you don't bring him to me, I'll slit his throat." Remi pulled a dagger from his waistband and positioned it under Athos's chin. Athos wriggled, but every attempt tightened the gypsy's pressure. The blade felt cool compared to the man's hatred.

Athos counted on Camille, huddled with Nicole, to make the right decision and bring Pierre up.

Camille returned to the passage below and disappeared. Nicole, rather than stay put, came within dueling distance of Remi.

"Stay away!" Athos pleaded and struggled to break free. But Nicole's determination stuck.

"Remi," she began, using her boundless compassion. "Did you hear what I told you about your son in the Gallery of Souls?"

Remi's chest rose and fell more quickly. "Sibonne."

"Do you know what happened to her?"

"Yes, but—" he said but stopped himself.

"She's gone."

Remi held the knife fast to Athos's throat. Any tighter and there'd be no room for error.

"She died of heartbreak, Remi. My husband caused it after he separated you two. But many of the details are unclear."

Remi's contempt wasn't. "I raised our son—my *dead* son— alone. The Comte never found us. All those years of tracking us, and he never came close."

"So you knew about Pierre?" Nicole finally understood. She gulped back the reality. "You sent us a decoy to stop the Comte's incessant hunt."

Remi's grimace turned to a snide grin. "And it threw him off our scent, for a while."

"I always thought Pierre was part of our family," she said. She could taste the remorse. "Who was he?"

Remi laughed coolly. "Just another mouth to feed among the gypsies, a wayward orphan who thought living with a rich man sounded better than competing among us for a bite to eat. He was too young to know any better."

*The unimaginable cruelty.* She struggled to start again. "Sibonne wrote letters to her real son. She probably counted on me reading them right away, after her death, but I didn't. I just read them today. I should have never waited.

"Remi," Nicole refocused, "Sibonne's son should have a birthmark behind his left ear. A teardrop. I knew instantly when I read this that Pierre didn't have one. So, when I saw you with your son, there was only one conclusion. Pierre had killed my real nephew."

Remi huffed. "And that, Madam, is what I will redeem." Remi looked over her shoulder to where Camille had disappeared.

Nicole placed herself in the way. "Your son doesn't have a birthmark either."

Remi shifted his eyes to hers, and Athos felt his captor loosen his grip, if only by the width of a blade. "Don't try to trick me, Comtesse. I've lived far too long with the best of liars."

"Doesn't it stand to reason that if he were my nephew, I, too, would also be overcome with grief?" She clasped her hands at her heart. "He's not the son of Sibonne. She's sending us a message from the grave."

"This is madness!" Remi said, releasing the knife to point at her. "You think I'm easily duped? You're quite mistaken!"

She pulled a folded paper from her pocket. "I brought the letter with me. To show Pierre. I don't think he read it, but you should."

The paper swallowed the space between them.

"Keep your letter. I know my own son. And he's gone, and soon, the fool who killed him will be, too."

Athos acted in that split second. Twisting his body, he ducked under Remi's hold and kneed him in the groin. Remi doubled over.

Athos rushed to Nicole and almost stumbled into her. He could not remember a time when a woman had rescued him.

Before the three could rebound from the power shuffle, intense clopping filled the marketplace. About a dozen horses overtook the area. A guard of the Cardinal's sat on every steed. They shouted at the three to surrender and drop their weapons, maneuvering until Athos, Nicole, and Remi were back-to-back with no room to spare. The excited horses danced around them, and the guardsmen hollered commands at each other until one man parted the way for a second set of riders.

Cardinal Richelieu, wearing his embroidered riding jacket, sat on a black horse in the lead. Space was made for him to dismount. The night air chilled as he walked toward them.

"You've caused me much consternation," he stated, turning a cold eye to each of them and lastly, Athos. "I should have you executed on the spot."

Athos held Nicole back by the elbows. The Cardinal's laugh swirled around the trio.

"My dear, your continued illicit behaviour leads you deeper into the depths of Hell. You, along with that bastard child of yours." He dropped his gaze to her midriff.

Nicole filled her chest, but Athos whispered to stay quiet. She pursed her lips.

"I have no punishment for you that God will not mete out in his own time. But these men," Richelieu said, motioning to Athos and Remi, "and the rest of your illicit crew, must be punished." From behind him, Camille, Pierre, and Jeanne appeared with their hands held behind their backs by guardsmen.

A satisfied smile undercut the Cardinal's sinister intent. "You three men in Le Prix have presented me with a dilemma. You've broken the rules against dueling and have incapacitated my own men. For this, you must pay with your lives."

The Cardinal snapped his fingers, and a man from his team untied a scroll and began to read.

"At the declaration of Cardinal Richelieu and the sacred Catholic Church of France, it is hereby declared that any captured competitors of Le Prix du Fer shall duel to the death in the square at Notre Dame in two nights hence of their capture. The winner of any said duel shall be publicly executed. No survivors shall be pardoned."

The man took the scroll and hammered it to a post in the marketplace.

"It seems fitting," the Cardinal said, mounting his horse, "that instead of a victor, there shall only be the dead. If Paris wants a show, it will have one."

# The Last Duel

In isolation at Jeanne's meager quarters, Nicole heard little news over the next day and a half. At the persuasive insistence of the red-head, the Cardinal had agreed to let them stay at the brothel, but even the fanciful and doting women in the house couldn't console Nicole. In exchange for performing lurid favours for their captors, Jeanne disappeared for hours at a time, only to return with small bites of food or a bottle of wine and the same news: "No word yet."

Nicole wasn't even sure what word would come. The Death Duel, as it had become known, was publicly announced the morning after their capture. Pierre, Remi, and Athos—the condemned—were jailed at unknown locations. Camille, who was considered the lesser offender because he hadn't entered Le Prix, stayed under house arrest at Athos's apartment at the Rue Férou, so even he couldn't send word to Nicole. More than anything, the news she wanted to hear was that the Cardinal had undergone a change of heart.

*Impossible.*

The night before the Death Duel, Jeanne returned with an unexpected visitor. She persuaded the guards to let him in under the ruse that Nicole needed a priest. Not so far from the truth.

Father Grignan placed a handful of pistachios in Nicole's palm following a prolonged hug.

"I'd lost hope of ever seeing you again," she said, teary-eyed. She gingerly placed the nuts in a pewter chalice, one of Jeanne's few possessions.

He nodded, raising a scarred eyebrow, and attempted a smile. "Everyone in the intrigue lost interest in the only person unwilling to duel." He pointed to himself, then the mischievous twinkle in his eyes faded, and he looked away. "We have no bargaining power."

Nicole gathered his hands and requested a prayer, which he quickly offered. She decided to reveal the secret about Pierre's background. There had been no time to tell Pierre the whole story during their escape.

"Would the truth make a difference to him now?" Grignan asked.

She took small comfort that it didn't. She hugged her middle. "How can the Cardinal do this? It defies his own decree."

"That's the beauty of being the Cardinal. No one—save the King—can rein him in, and even that fact is often debatable."

The room quieted.

"What can we do?" Nicole worried over a rosary the priest handed her. She sighed and sat in the only chair in Jeanne's room, one meant for a kitchen table. Grignan lowered himself to one knee beside her.

"You must prepare," he said. His grave tone gave her no allusions of hope. "I'm doing my best to convince the Cardinal's underlings to allow me to offer the men last rites."

Oblivious, Jeanne chimed in, running her words together. "If we could gather the Musketeers, couldn't they break up the duel? Start a measly?"

"A melee?" Grignan said, puzzling over the energetic young woman to whom scheming seemed natural.

"Musketeers don't like the Cardinal and his guards anyway," she said, "so what's not to like about that idea?"

"Plenty," Grignan said, taking to his feet. He crossed to the window where he parted a thin curtain and glared at the guards below. "There's very little stomach among the guardsmen to fight each other in an all-out war."

Jeanne shook her mop of curly red hair. "But they duel all the time ..."

"Because duels are about honour. They do so to defend their reputations. Le Prix is something different and not necessarily an honourable pursuit. That's why so few guards enter."

"But they always earn the most applause," Jeanne said with a little huff.

"That's because the people love them. Well, most of them. Le Prix is really only about hubris."

"What-bris?" Jeanne asked.

"Hubris: unbridled, glorified egotism," he answered.

"The Musketeers would step in and fight for other reasons." Jeanne cracked a pistachio, popped it in her mouth, and took a good look out the window, too. "Men always have a weakness."

∞∞∞

The morning of the duel at dawn, guards transported Nicole and Jeanne to the square of Notre Dame. A fine mist circulated in the city air. The sun struggled to shine through a cloud. Already, the mood defied that of Le Prix. Heaviness overshadowed revelry.

A drab circular stage had been erected overnight near the entrance of the Cathedral of Notre Dame, and soon spectators formed clusters at the best vantage points. Whether this outdid Le Prix was debatable, and everyone seemed to be debating. If death sports weren't the favourite pastime of Parisians, then arguing was.

Grignan arrived alone but stood within Nicole's line of sight, though too far to easily communicate. Two guards stood on either side of the women.

The stage, worn and buckled, was typically used for executions; the only props missing were an axeman in black and a chopping block. The crowd grew larger about the time an embellished carriage arrived in front of a sturdier raised platform near the side of the stage. In far better shape than the main stage, the viewing platform was draped in shiny swags of heavy red cloth. Gold rope-ties pulled the swags to the edges, and a square flag with the insignia of the Cardinal hung from the front rail.

First from the carriage emerged the Cardinal's envoys dressed in robes of brown felted wool. Then the Cardinal, a statuesque figure in formal attire, arose behind the group. His crisp white cuffs and collar gave him the air of perfection and power. His emotionless expression conveyed confidence.

Once Richelieu was positioned at the centre of the viewing platform, several of the Cardinal's guards moved across the stage. One unfurled a parchment. By now, spectators were shoulder to shoulder, exhibiting little excitement of any kind, unlike Le Prix. No small French flags. No singing. No celebratory shouts. The ocean of faces waited to see the doomed.

A lock clattered, and the front doors of the cathedral rumbled open. One by one the offenders marched up a short set of steps onto the stage, hands tied behind their backs. One guard led the way, and another tailed the men.

Face-forward, the men were lined up across the rear of the stage. The three captors stood at five-foot intervals from left to right—Athos, Pierre, and Remi. The older men held expressions of lethal resolve, Pierre being the exception. Pale and hollowed out, he stared flatly ahead.

Nicole clasped her hands so tightly that even her short prayer could not escape. Was it possible? Pierre looked worse than ever, gaunt, beaten-down, disheveled. Shadows encircled his blank eyes; his facial injuries from Remi's beating showed few signs of healing. His hands, missing two digits and one peeling, were unbandaged. He was in no shape to stand upright, let alone fight.

Three swords, stuck tip-down in the planks at center stage, glistened in the oncoming daylight. Apparently, a scramble for a weapon would start the Death Duel.

The guard with the parchment stepped in front of the weapons and cleared his throat before he read from the scroll.

"By the decree of Cardinal Richelieu of the Kingdom of France and the sacred Catholic Church, these men are hereby charged with defying the ban against dueling. As fitting punishment, they shall duel to the death until none or one is left standing. Any survivor will be beheaded. So it shall be."

A murmur passed through the crowd. Overcome, Nicole buried her head in Jeanne's shoulder. "I cannot watch." But she had no choice. Her punishment included witnessing the match. A guard jerked her chin forward.

Jeanne patted her back. "Don't worry, madam. I'd wager the real show won't be a swordfight."

∞∞∞

The drumbeat of Athos's heart filled his chest.

Every beat embodied his father, his mother, his Nicole, his unborn son. Their names vibrated up his spine and between his temples. His imminent demise seemed inescapable.

*I must kill. Or be killed.*

His suicidal leap from the tavern rooftop over a year ago suddenly felt foolish. Death by choice seemed an indulgence. Now, death without liberty trampled his hope. It took on the shape of the beast and triggered his darkest impulses: survive by any means. *Kill. Or be killed.*

The guards released his arms. Knives cut the ties at his wrists.

The man with the scroll boomed: "Let the duel begin!"

Athos's muscles fired.

He sprinted like lightning and reached the swords first.

Speed equaled advantage. Calculation equaled advantage. Precision equaled advantage. His hand found a pommel. He pulled the sword free and pointed it forward. If he killed one man, the death could psychologically conquer the other. Victory, a swipe closer.

But his heart was not in it. Especially killing Pierre. The last remnants of the once-vibrant young man had all but disappeared during their short, brutal confinement. In Athos's case, no food had come the last two days, and successive taunting guardsmen had thrashed him to keep him from sleep.

As Athos stood his last ground, Pierre and Remi retreated with their weapons, equidistant, cornered. Pierre was the last to find footing, so diminished was his strength. They concealed their fear, mere bulls-eyes waiting to be scored.

Poised to attack, Athos saw himself in them. He knew exactly what they were thinking. *How will I win? Which maneuver stands a chance? Will I be lucky and survive the last duel or find the fortitude to hide my agony when death comes? Which is better? To die by the sword now? Or by the ax or rope later?*

As a Musketeer, every fight had been an opportunity for his last. His fatalism ruled though never bore out. Yet not once in all his years defending the King had he been commanded to make death a show.

*Now I'm only a pawn.*

He snatched the next beat of his heart, slowed his pulse, moved back several steps, widened the divide between his baser instincts and his higher self, and slowly laid down his sword.

He faced the masses below and roared: "No more!"

∞∞∞∞

Nicole snapped her eyes open. Never in a millennium was this possible.

"I told you so," Jeanne said, a cat-like smugness rounding her words.

"No more!" he shouted again, though the crowd remained hushed. Arms extended in truce, he turned toward the Cardinal, who stood eerily still. "I'm done fighting. This is preposterous. A mockery. You're setting a despicable precedent for your people. All of them!"

Athos swept his arms forward and viewed the audience from end to end. Behind him, a nervous shuffling began. If Pierre, Remi, or the guards subdued him now, they'd never hear his final message.

"No Musketeer has withstood as long as my tenure. I've seen friends and enemies slain in front of me, because of me. Death always wins. *It lasts forever.* I will succumb to it one day, maybe before the sun sets tonight, but I refuse to bring about anyone's last breath ever again. I lay down my sword forever. I've done my duty, and now I must honour my conscience. Absolution will be mine," he stared at the Cardinal, "whether you grant it or not."

Nicole sucked in a short breath and caught a glimpse of Grignan crossing himself. The quiet throughout the square chilled Nicole's bones. Even Jeanne seemed to be holding her breath, enrapt. Then, she did something that struck Nicole as boldly defiant. Jeanne started to chant.

"Free these men! Free these men!"

A few peasants around them joined in. Soon, the chant spread, and within seconds, every wide-eyed face carried the message. Fists were pumped. Kids were lifted from the ground. A buoyancy transformed the mood from doom to determination. The Cardinal's eyes darted between Athos and the audience as a growing unease creased his brow.

"Free these men! Free these men!"

Nicole found her voice. It came out parched at first, but Jeanne's smile and enthusiasm rejuvenated it. For endless minutes, by collective ambition, the chanting lifted the crowd.

Athos stepped aside for the vocal wave, growing stronger as the Cardinal's confidence visibly crumpled. The pontiff jerked his head and shouted commands at one envoy then another, but confusion ensued. No one knew what to do. Several guardsmen surrounded the base of the platform and yelled at the nearby crowd to get away. Few complied.

The scuffle behind Athos sharpened. Steel blades clanged aggressively. He spun around to find Remi in full combat with Pierre.

∞∞∞∞

An incessant ringing drained Pierre of his last energy. His recent torture had eroded his physical capacity. The days of captivity since Le Prix had emptied him. Whippings. Vices. Knives. Unholy pain. Agony beyond evil.

Like Remi's attacks, despair swept over him like an avalanche.

He was without ground, a nothing, a blank.

He would never be a Musketeer.

His fidelity to Hannah was ruined.

His daughter was beyond reach.
His family history, despicable.
Mind, diseased.
Body, broken.
All he possessed was a sword.

∞∞∞

Athos immediately recognizing the dark disconnect when he reached Pierre to defend him. His friend had fractured. Even Athos couldn't help.

In fact, his mere presence jolted Pierre into an illogical rage.

"Pierre, no!" Athos deflected Pierre's assaults while Remi stood back, awaiting the outcome or an opening. The crowd's chanting slowed to a halt and murmurs wound through the stirring pockets of people.

"I'm dead already. We both are," Pierre declared emotionlessly. "You can't save me no matter how hard you try. It's over."

In sloppy swipes, Pierre's energy flagged, but he kept swinging at Athos like an angry child.

In the intensifying disarray, Remi kicked Athos's feet from underneath him and attacked Pierre again. The gypsy was no contest. Pierre stumbled and fell to a knee, his sword held weakly above his head. Remi battered, again and again, swinging with viscous focus, causing Pierre to buckle onto both knees with only an arm shielding his face. Athos scrambled up and dove sword-first, but the fatal blow arrived before the Musketeer did.

Remi's sword opened the side of Pierre's neck. Blood sprayed in every direction. Streaks of red covered the blade and splattered Remi's hands and Athos's face. Screams laced through the crowd.

Pierre fell hard and lurched in one spasm off the back of the wooden stage and out of sight.

In a single leap, Athos, stunned and unable to think, landed next to him. His was the kind of death Athos hated most. Nothing could be done. Pressure on the wound wouldn't prolong the outcome, no last words would be spoken, no sacrament given, no legacy laid out. Just desperate rapid gasps and gushes of blood. The eyes were the hardest to watch. They bulged in utter terror. Athos held his apprentice firmly, eye-to-eye, cradling his head. After the last gurgle for air, Athos bent over the blood-soaked body and laid hands on his friend for the last time.

# 24

# The Aftermath

**M**inutes later, covered in blood, Athos blockaded Nicole from reaching the back of the stage.

"No, you mustn't," he insisted.

The situation outside Notre Dame escalated to chaos. Musketeers poured into the stone square from all directions, picking fights with dozens of Cardinal's guards. Onlookers were taking sides, placing bets, and tossing rotten produce and small sticks at Richelieu's carriage, where he had sequestered himself. His team of horses whinnied and pitched while guards tried subduing them, unable to clear a path from the mayhem.

Nicole sobbed inconsolably. Grignan, at her side, had delivered her to Athos after Jeanne distracted their guards. "That woman has an impeccable knack for thinking on her feet," the priest said, marveling at the teeming result.

"Is he ...?" Nicole grabbed Athos by the collar. Her eyes were already puffy and bloodshot.

Athos hugged her again, despite the blood. "We must find a way out of here," he urged and grabbed her hand tightly, peering over the bobbing heads in all directions.

"Do you think Jeanne had anything to do with these Musketeers showing up?" Grignan asked, still puzzling over the explosive situation.

Heading away from the carriage and stage, Athos didn't hesitate to respond. "It wouldn't surprise me."

Nicole pulled Athos into her. "We can't leave him," she said. Such beautiful mercy, he thought.

He kissed her softly and spoke as if they were alone rather than in the midst of a melee masterminded by a clever peasant. "My love," he began, taking another kiss, "Pierre lives here." He kissed the back of her hand and laid it on his heart. "We must go on without him. Time is of the essence. He would want your safety first."

She dropped her chin to her chest, and he pressed his lips onto her forehead. "I'll never forget him," he added, squeezing her hands. Her shoulders fell, and she let out another weepy shudder.

He turned his attention to Grignan. "What of Remi?"

"He ran off. From where I stood, it looked like he saw an opportunity and took it."

Athos nodded and maneuvered through the barrier of excited people. He set his sights on a grouping of Musketeers far from the worst commotion. Their blue tabards stood out in the crowd.

Pushing and nudging, Athos bettered their position without drawing excessive notice. Close to the Musketeers' huddle, he lost Nicole's hand. Grignan had disappeared as well. Straining to look behind him, his heart sank.

Ten paces behind, Vachon held her. Jostling to clear a way, Athos discovered he had her by the middle, a knife at her belly.

She fidgeted against his hold, but fear raced in her eyes.

Of this, Athos was absolutely certain: they would never be rid of him unless it ended here.

Vachon shoved Nicole forward. She whimpered and took a small step, then another.

"No one will ever know who killed you in this hysteria." His maniacal stare told Athos what he already knew. The ones with grudges always proved the last to go down.

"You risk your benefactor's newly acquired wealth," Athos said. "Geneviève will be most displeased if you kill us and she loses her sovereignty."

Vachon laughed so loudly that a few troublemakers next to him chuckled along.

"In this crowd? How would anyone know? I'm sure there'll be more than one dead Musketeer today."

"Leave Nicole out of it then. If you want revenge, kill me."

"And ruin the family fun?"

Athos had only his bare hands. He needed a sword. "Duel me," Athos challenged, "in exchange for her freedom."

Athos's skin crawled at Vachon's contemptuous grin. The villain squeezed Nicole's windpipe shut, and her face immediately turned pink. Vachon shouted into the frenzy. "Swords! Two swords here!"

Athos struggled to get within arm's length. Nicole clawed at Vachon's hand around her throat, but he wasn't budging. Athos moved so near, he could smell his foul breath. "You're just like your brother. Reckless," Athos seethed. "Let her go."

Faking a bow, Vachon released Nicole from the strangle and sheathed the knife behind him. Nicole fell into Athos's arms and wheezed for air. He embraced her gently, careful to keep an eye on the man who wanted them dead.

"Don't worry," Vachon said. "I won't stab you in the back like Pierre killed my brother. I'd much rather watch your life drain away when I run you through."

It didn't take long for the impending fight to attract the attention of the nearby Musketeers. Six surrounded the two men, including Longdac, a sight for sore eyes.

Pulling Athos aside, Longdac offered, "We could easily take him."

Nicole nodded and grabbed Athos by the shoulders. "You cannot fight him," she rasped. "I forbid it. You said 'no more' and made a promise to yourself and your countrymen. You can't break it."

He wanted to believe the better part of him meant his word. Yet Vachon stood to stalk their future. "My word is my word. And my word was to duel in exchange for your freedom. He granted it, and my pact is made."

Nicole shook her head vigorously. "This isn't your fight. It's Pierre's." She faltered on his name. Would it destroy her to see a second loved one killed in the same day? After all they'd been through, was he capable of winning?

Vachon's patience expired. "Renege, and I'll make both your lives a living Hell."

Athos tore himself from Nicole's hold and instructed Longdac, "Keep her back and the crowd at bay. Don't intervene."

Swords made their way to each man, and they spared formalities.

Athos lunged instantaneously, hoping to offset Vachon's confidence. His solid block foretold otherwise. Vachon demonstrated strength and focus. He'd been priming for this fight, or one like it with Pierre, for almost a year. He wasn't going to go down easily.

Peasants tightened the circle around the men. Longdac and his Musketeers blockaded them. The limited space deterred momentum. Athos's attacks lacked power. Clumsy at best, dangerously weak at worst. Vachon mounted quicker counter-attacks, allowing little time before taking the offensive. Athos's recoveries grew slower and sloppier.

It didn't help that Nicole stood so close.

"Get her out of here," Athos finally shouted at Longdac.

"No!" she responded but finally relented when Longdac stood like a mountain in front of her.

Her distraction had diminished his precious energy. Vachon taunted him. "You're weak and old, Athos. Everyone sees it."

Athos pushed the words out of his mind. Every clang of their swords reminded him of his long brutal history. Each fight had taken its toll. A little more of his body and mind broke down with every conflict. The scars marked his skin and spirit. The lack of care had exacted a price.

The fight stretched on, but the intensity waned. Vachon, though the stronger man, breathed heavily. Sweat drenched Athos's back. Their sparring turned loose and shapeless. After one close call, Athos lost his balance and fell backward into the crowd, forcing a slight pause in the fight. Many offered a hands-up, but their pity agitated him.

"Get back!" Athos yelled. The peasants helped anyway.

His bad shoulder ached, his back burned from lashings, his stamina ran dry. Dueling used to feed him energy; now it drained him. His body floundered.

But not his mind. His mind stayed keen.

*Strength is no match for cunning.*

The next time he fell, he went straight into Vachon's stomach.

The two landed in a heap, Athos topside. He pinned Vachon down by the elbows. Vachon wrestled, but Athos, the heftier, didn't give an inch.

"This is not a duel!" Vachon spat at him.

"But it is a means to survival." Athos nodded to Longdac to grab his stray sword. "His throat."

Longdac stuck the tip under Vachon's chin, rendering him useless.

"You dishonourable wretch!" The veins in Vachon's neck bulged. "Stand with your sword, coward!"

"Why? So you can feel good about this? Vachon, I want to live. And I don't necessarily want to kill you to do it."

"I'll never relent!"

Athos needn't have said another word. Slowly, Vachon noticed every soul in the periphery staring at him. "I heard your damnable speech, such enlightened dribble! You'll always be a killer."

Catching Athos slightly off balance, Vachon slipped his knife from the sheath beneath him and buried the weapon deeply into Athos's thigh. Longdac reacted by instinct and instantly sliced Vachon's throat. In simultaneous precision, his life spilled away and his voice died, too.

Racked with pain and bleeding profusely, Athos writhed off the dead man and clenched his thigh. With the help of several Musketeers, Longdac quickly steadied Athos and pulled the knife free.

# The Long Road Home

The days following the debacle ran together like watercolor on a damp canvas. Athos did everything in his power to buffer Nicole, who suffered Pierre's death poorly. The week following the melee, they were summoned to appear before King Louis and explain their involvement. Him, for defying the decree against dueling; her, for aiding a criminal.

Athos successfully argued that the Cardinal's contrived punishment at Notre Dame made a mockery of the ban against duels. Louis, indulging his infinite admiration of Athos, pardoned him on the promise that his dueling days were over. Athos assured the King they were, and he officially signed a resignation from his post. He reclaimed some of his dignity when he overheard Louis tell a minister, "I'll miss him."

Nicole wasn't as fortunate. She and Father Grignan were censured for aiding Pierre. Because of their intent, the King said,

Pierre had escaped from the Bastille and instigated trouble from the moment he hit the streets. To Father Grignan's credit, the priest insisted the escape was a solo venture with no support from the former Comtesse. And, he argued, the offending party was dead. Plus, it was learned that Jeanne, Pierre's counterpart in disgrace, had been captured and sent to a nunnery. These last facts seemed to satisfy the need for justice. Nicole and the priest were sent on their way, but not before the King had one last question, though rhetorical. "Did you truly relinquish *all* of your wealth?"

The most difficult part of the royal punishment was their departure from Le Louvre. After the hearings, scores of French nobles formed a gauntlet through the halls. The crowd included Geneviève. Some jeered at the trio as they passed. Others issued condescending jibes. As soon as they made it out, Nicole vowed never to step foot in Le Louvre again.

The degradation, combined with Pierre's death, caused her to mentally retreat. For days in d'Artagnan's apartment, where they'd taken up temporary residence, she refused to eat or talk. Athos understood she wasn't upset at him but disturbed by the injustice of their circumstance.

Needing respite as well, he simply stayed close to her and admired her round belly and soft features. He wrote her poetry and read it aloud. She eventually came around. Before they could leave Paris for good, several matters needed attention. Chiefly, they had to decide where to call home.

"We cannot go back to Rochefort," Nicole told him.

Athos glazed over at the streetview below the apartment. His thigh ached constantly, and her fatigue kept them grounded. They'd been resting for three weeks since the Death Duel.

"My castle, Bragelonne," he said, "you'll find to your liking." He wondered when d'Artagnan might return, when all the preparations would be finalized for their departure, and when better days stood to outnumber the bad.

"Tell me about it." She snuggled into the down-filled bedding. He'd made sure they had a better, bigger bed in place for their convalescence.

"You'll have fresh fruit from the orchards, clear skies, space to roam." It seemed so long ago since their days enjoying the lush hillsides on her estate.

"When were you there last?"

He sent her a soft grin from across the room and shook his head. "I've never been."

"What?"

"It's a long story, one for another time." He returned to lie beside her. His mood was on the upswing because her frailty seemed to be subsiding. The longer they stayed out of the public eye, the better she felt.

"My magistrate, Bronte, will tend to our every need," he reassured her. It had been years since he'd seen his oldest friend, prior to becoming a Musketeer.

Nicole stared at the ceiling. "Hannah said in her letter that the staff will be ready to leave by month's end. I dread telling her."

*Pierre is gone.*

"Hannah and baby Sophia are lucky to have you," Athos said.

Arrangements for Pierre's body took place before they even stepped foot before the King. Grignan had been their savior. Again. While Athos battled Vachon, the priest had doubled-back for the body to keep the beggars and crows from disassembling it. A sympathetic friend in the Cathedral secured it inside Notre Dame until they could transport the body to Rochefort, where his mother was buried.

Well, not his real mother. "I wish I could have had more time with him," Nicole repeated. Her hand grazed Athos's cheek. The light in the apartment began to dim from the quickening dusk.

"He always held you in high esteem. He wanted you to be safe, Nicole. I think he felt responsible for many of the bad things that happened because of his poor decisions."

"I know, but he never knew who he was."

"Like a Greek tragedy," he said. "All his life had been one."

"I wonder, if somewhere in France, my true nephew lives on?" She contemplated the idea, a cloud in her eyes.

"Perhaps," Athos said, rubbing a wrinkle from her brow.

Her hands ran across the bedsheets and up the rise of her belly. Then she leaned over for a kiss.

"I love you," she said.

"And I, you."

THE END

# Epilogue

The day before their departure from Paris, in a small chapel at Saint Germain-de-Prés, beneath the statue of Saint Benoit, Athos and Nicole exchanged vows. Father Simon Grignan conducted the mass. Camille was their only witness. Three months later, at the Castle de Bragelonne, Nicole gave birth to a son. They named him Raoul.

# Acknowledgment

Thank you to Musketeer lovers everywhere and to my sympathetic readers and encouraging fans. The end was written because of you.

**www.TheMusketeerSeries.com**